The Back & Forth
OF A WOMAN'S
LOVE

SONNY D. STONE

OTHER PUBLICATIONS BY SONNY

Jenna Lee Series
The Ups and Downs of a Woman's Heart, Book 1
The Ins and Outs of a Woman's Dream, Book 2

Publishing Coordinator – Sharon Kizziah-Holmes
Cover Design – Jaycee DeLorenzo

INDIE PUB PRESS

an imprint of A & S Publishing
A & S Holmes, Inc.

ISBN 13: 978-1-956806-00-7

DEDICATION

Sharon Stone thank you for your love and support throughout the writing process. Your proofing, and ideas really added to the fun of the journey.

To my family and friends thank you for being there for me. Steve, if you hadn't continually pushed me in the publishing direction, these books would still be sitting in my computer. Thank you for your patient and loving contributions. Stan thanks for all you do to make life so great. Greg and Jackie, the two of you bless me with encouragement, joy, and laughter.

ACKNOWLEDGMENTS

Thank you to my publishing coordinator Sharon, who has been available for calls, texts, e-mails, and meetings. Thank you for your years of service with Jenna's trilogy.

Chapter 1

Newlyweds

Jacob and I have been married for nine months and I moved across the country from Missouri to Kentucky to live with my off the charts hot husband. Jacob was born and raised here in Kentucky, and his international business hub and all his family were here too.

Before we got married, he'd built the dream home that is now our happy home. He is very hard working and reaps the benefits of being a successful business entrepreneur. He has hundreds of acres of land and sells prime hay and alfalfa to livestock owners all over the world. He has internet sites for his other business ventures too, but his hay business is his baby, and I'm very proud of his vision and management skills.

Jacob is loving, kind and provides generously for me financially. I gave up my teaching career and home in Missouri to build a life with my childhood friend who grew into an amazing man. Every morning I wake up next to him and remind myself that I'm not dreaming because my husband is better than I ever could imagine. When we walk together hand in hand in public, women turn to watch him. I can't blame them because he is so beautiful. He says that I get just as many men turning to see me, but he's just being kind to say that, it's totally not true. I have this secret fear that one morning he's going to wake up, and without any warning realize he's made a big mistake marrying me, and I'm going to be without the man of my dreams. I just try to enjoy each day like it's a gift, because when it boils down to it, that's all we really have any way, one day at a time.

After packing most of my personal belongings, I sent some of my things to my mom, and then gave lots of my stuff, furniture, clothes, and my kitchen items to the local women's shelter. Then I scheduled the Disabled Veterans organization to come pick up the rest of my household items so Jacob wouldn't have to store my belongings in his warehouse any longer than he already had.

His house, I mean our house is a large log cabin, with wooden floors, some curved wooden walls, but mostly sheetrock white walls. Our place is minimalistic, but he's encouraged me to put my touches of color and a few floral print pillows here and there if I wanted to. His only request, no frilly sequences and no pink, so I could feel at home at our place too.

I quickly added accent pillows of reds and yellows. At one point we thought that we might be pregnant, so Jacob immediately started plans to build a large room onto the house. After I lost the baby, Jacob offered to make the new room into a photography studio for me to develop my interest in photography and make me feel like I have a personal space in our home too. I was taking a photography class that I really enjoyed and was dating my instructor when Jacob and I were on a "break."

My favorite part of our home is the wrap around porch. We have two rocking chairs on every side of the house. We go out in the early morning or in the cool of the evening and have a cup of coffee and enjoy the beautiful rolling hills and horses. It is beautiful here with the miles and miles of deep green grassy fields framed with miles of white fences.

I've taken many photos of the amazing sunrises and sunsets I've seen with my husband on his land. Every once in a while, a herd of deer come close to the house. There are salt licks on both the east and west sides of the house for deer to feed and water on the west side of the house for them. I've tried to capture the beauty of Kentucky in photographs, but it's just not the same as seeing the real thing. The fresh air, the cool evening and morning breeze, cup of coffee, husband by my side, my slice of heaven. I can't think of a better way to start or end my days.

On the career front, I've applied for every teaching position and principal position within a 45-minute drive from where I live. But in small town rural communities, jobs don't come available very often. I was told I could work as a substitute and see if any positions would become available for the future.

One principal had the nerve to say I should have my husband build a new school and I could manage that one. I guess he wasn't a big fan of my husband's money and power in the community. Long story short, I didn't feel hopeful that my teaching career would be reengaged in Kentucky.

I did get an encouraging call for a job interview on campus at the university to teach teachers how to teach kindergarten. I was really excited about this employment opportunity. I hadn't been to this campus before. Security requires every car driving onto campus have a pass to get onto campus during the school day.

Jacob was familiar with the area and drove me around to see the campus the night before my interview. That way I would know exactly where to go, where to park, and how to find the building I was supposed to be in for the interview. The next morning Jacob and I had our coffee together on our porch, and he headed for work and I headed out excited and hopeful for my job interview.

I drove right to where I needed to be, got the pass to get on campus, parked on the main street just down half a block from the building for my interview and walked to the office for my meeting. I met with the head of the education department, and several elementary education teachers. They asked me several questions and I thought I did really well with the interview and with making personal connections. I was really excited that this was a good fit for me and a new chapter in my professional life.

They wanted me to go back to school and get my doctorate. I told them if they hired me, I'd be glad to do that as my teaching schedule allowed. They said I was the last candidate being interviewed and that I would hear back from them in the next two to three days. I thanked each one by name, which was impressive to me because I'm terrible at remembering names. I remember faces but names usually escape me.

Walking out to my car I was feeling pretty pumped that my interview went so well. I was going over the interview in my mind with a smile on my face when I got to my car. I stopped in shock and horror. I couldn't believe what I saw. My new car was trashed.

I immediately called Jacob, got him out of a meeting and said "I just finished my interview and I'm at my car and someone broke into my car. It looks like someone took a crowbar and opened the drivers' side door, and then it looks like they dumped a large trash bag of trash inside my car. Why would someone do that? What should I do?"

"Call the campus police and I'll be there as soon as I can get to you."

"You don't need to come unless my car won't start, but I just wanted you to know, I just can't believe it."

4

"I'm coming to you so don't worry, it will be okay. Call the campus police and let them know what happened. Don't touch anything in case they need finger prints, or whatever. I love you Jenna, just stay calm. I'll be there soon."

I walked back inside to the office secretary and asked her if she had the phone number to campus police. She gave me the number I thanked her and walked back out to my car. As I was walking back out to the car, the head of the education department called my name in the hallway.

"Jenna, is everything okay? My secretary said you needed the police."

"I'm okay, thanks for asking. It appears that someone has broken into my car while I was in the interview. Not only that they trashed the inside of my car."

"Wow, that's crazy! I'm so sorry that happened to you. That never happens here". He walked out with me to my car as we waited for the campus police to arrive. But as we were standing there, he asked me a really good question.

"Didn't you say in your interview that this was your first time on campus?"

"Yes, I did, why do you ask?

"Because this car has a campus sticker on the back bumper of the car, so this cannot be your car."

I walked out into the middle of the street in semi-disbelief to what he just said and at that moment I could see the campus police pulling up to my location out of the corner of my eye. Then as I looked behind what I thought was my car, there was a large white moving van and behind this big white moving van was my car. Oh my gosh, I have the wrong car! How embarrassing!

I looked at Dr. LeeClusey, shaking my head in shocked amazement and said, "Joe, it looks like I just made my interview memorable. I'm so embarrassed for mistaking my car. I guess I was nervous from the interview and didn't check my surroundings well enough."

The police officer walked up to me and I explained I

made a big mistake, and all was well. Dr. LeeClusey excused himself, I'm sure he couldn't wait to get back to the office and tell them what a space cadet I was.

I called Jacob to tell him. "Jacob, it's all a mistake. It's not my car. Sorry to have taken you away from work. I'm going to head home now." Jacob didn't even have words to respond to me. Not good. "I must have been stressed from my interview. It was an honest mistake."

"Just drive safe and I am going to turn around and go back to work." *I cannot believe she did that. She just threw any chances she had for that job down the toilet.*

"Thanks for coming even though it was a false alarm. Glad to know I can always count on you. Love you."

"Love you too. See you later tonight."

Unfortunately, later I found out that I did not get the job and I really wanted it. A couple of weeks had past, since my job interview catastrophe, and I finally had the courage to go back and show my face in the area. I navigated my way in this college town to my favorite coffee house, to meet my new good friend Larry and his girlfriend Lanna.

He once again was encouraging me to take more photography classes at the local university. "Where have you been lately?"

"It's a long story, you better get your coffee and have a seat first." Then I told him about my interview. He laughed a solid ten minutes before he could regain his composure. People were looking at us and laughing with us even though they had no idea why we or they were laughing.

Glad so many could enjoy my painful experience. By the time he finally finished laughing at my interview debacle, I was laughing too. It was good to finally be able to laugh at myself. I'd felt so foolish about it that I hadn't just let it go, so now it's hopefully gone. What was funny was to hear Larry try to retell the coffee patrons what we were laughing at. Everyone really cracked up when they knew why he was laughing so hard.

The coffeehouse manager came to the table and gave me a card. He said, "the next ten coffees are free. That was the best interview story I've ever heard. I've conducted many interviews and that tops them all."

"Thank you! I will use this because I think I'm going to be called that "Interview woman" from now on." Now that we were all laughing at me, I could see the humor from their perspective.

I remember asking Jacob what he told his employees about my job interview, and he said "nothing, I told them I had to leave on a pressing matter." When I got about ten miles out of town you called me. I just turned around and went back to work.

Jacob never offered anything supportive or questioning about the incident ever again. Jacob doesn't have a tolerance for stupid, and what I did, fell into that category in a big way! I hate it when I disappoint him, I could see it in his eyes. I told him I was sorry for the mix up and taking him away from his work. He just said, "it's over, forget about it and move on."

Now I have lots of free time and I am bored. You can only clean the house and work in the yard so long. I've managed to plant flowers around the house and planted vegetables in a couple raised gardens. My dogs love me being home all the time, but even they sleep most the time we are together. Whatever I find to do, it just doesn't seem to be enough for me.

I call my mom and girlfriends back home, but they aren't long visits because they all ask, "what have you been doing?" I don't want to say, can't find a job, so I sit around and feel sorry for myself. Jacob works ten to twelve hours each day.

I'm filling my void; I've decided to take Larry's suggestion and go back to school. I had dated my last photography professor and almost married him, so Jacob wanted to meet the new photography instructor before I took his class, Jacob's so funny.

The instructor was nice looking actually, and I can see how some might think he's handsome, but he didn't hold a candle to my magazine cover husband. Jacob didn't actually meet him, but I'm sure he pulled him up on the computer and checked his credentials. I was taking an advanced photography class that met every Monday, Wednesday, and Friday at 10:00 to 11:30 in the morning. I loved the class, and the students that were taking the course were taking it because they wanted professional careers in photography too.

The classroom atmosphere was always serious and intense but creative and fun too. My last photography class was more like the instructors personality, very encouraging and supportive and personally helpful and more comfortable and laid back. I missed my old instructor and friend. I would love to tell him I'm taking photography classes again, he would be glad for me, but that's the type of man Brandon was and is. I miss him, but could never tell that to my husband or anyone else for that matter.

Now that I was busy again taking classes and focusing on photography, I felt happier, like I had some direction again. My husband was busy working deals and making money. His business was requiring more and more of his time, and I was feeling the sting of being the one in our marriage who made all the drastic changes to make our marriage work. I feel like something is missing when I'm not with Jacob. My photography class helps me fill my time but, it reminds me of my old instructor and friends all that much more.

Jacob and I see each other for breakfast and bed at night. But our quality time together, other than our sex life, was really missing from our relationship, especially that last few months. He had his life, his business and he had me on call, his life was full.

Mine had only Jacob and everything else was lacking. Even my enjoyment of photography didn't totally fill the void. Jacob wanted me to get out and make new friends, but the women my age had kids and were busy doing the mom things. The younger women wanted to get drunk at different clubs and although it's entertaining, it's not something I'd want to do every day and night.

My friend Larry and his girlfriend Lanna were fun to get together with. We'd go out sometimes when I was in town for classes, and I really liked Larry. He's very funny and kind. His girlfriend however is sort of self-absorbed and I didn't like the way she treated Larry.

Jacob was supposed to meet us for dinner and dancing for a Friday night date night, but he was late as usual. So, Larry, Lanna and I went ahead and ordered food at 7:00 and by 8:30 I said, "let's just go on to the club and have fun. Jacob may or may not join us, he works late a lot, but I can have fun with or without him."

Larry put his girlfriend under one arm and me under his other, and we walked down the street to the dance club. We were laughing and talking and enjoying the night air. The club had two bands playing that night. It was really booming a truly fun atmosphere and a fun get away.

I had rebroken my ankle on my honeymoon and had complications with it healing. I try to pay special attention to my surroundings when at a new place because my ankle is still weak. Dancing will be mild and purposeful not crazy fun.

I packed a short red dress and black heels for my date night with my husband who was missing in action. I texted Jacob to tell him the name of the club, if he ever got free, he could join us. I didn't even bother to ask him when he was coming, because it was always later than what he said

9

anyway. I was used to that ongoing disappointment.

Larry paid the cover charge for Lanna, and him. I walked up and the door man stamped my hand and didn't charge me, how sweet was that! I asked Larry if he paid for me, and he said no sorry, and I told him no problem, I just got in free.

He smiled and said, "no kidding, you are beautiful." Lanna smacked him in the arm and was staring daggers at me and him. Larry quickly said, "Jenna, I'm taking my best girl to the dance floor. We'll catch up with you in a few."

They danced and I assured him I'd be fine. Go enjoy. "I'll get us a table." I would have thanked him for the kind words but didn't want to say anything to upset his girlfriend. I found a table and before I had my butt in the chair, there was a nice-looking man with a drink in his hand headed my way. I thought, I am wearing a wedding ring, and if Jacob was here, I wouldn't have to have to deal with this stand-in for Jacob, but until he gets here, I'm having fun.

Rick was visiting his daughter at college and she wanted him to meet her friends. One of the girls was dating a boy in the band, so he was here with his daughter and her friends.

"Nice to meet you Rick. I'm Jenna Jamison. I was supposed to be on a date night with my husband, but he stood me up. I've decided to have fun without him."

"I'd be pleased to give you a spin on the dance floor if you want to dance."

Larry and Lanna came up to the table laughing and all smiles. I introduced Rick, and he proceeded to escort me out to the dance floor. The music was fast, and it felt great to cut loose and just have fun. I was enjoying the band, the atmosphere and dancing. We danced a couple of dances and then a slow song came on.

He didn't ask me, he just pulled me close to him. I didn't feel comfortable with that, so I was pushing away from him. He didn't take my strong suggestion. I spoke over the music, "Rick I want to set this one out."

He said "no, I want to feel you up next to me, believe me you won't be disappointed."

"Rick please, release me now." Just then I looked to my left and Jacob and Larry were standing right next to me. My heart jumped, and I froze. Jacob was not smiling, and he took my hand and leaned down and said something to Rick in a strong tone.

Rick just yelled over the music, "if you can't take good care of your woman, I'll do it for you buddy." I was afraid that Jacob was going to hit him, but he just laughed in his face and walked me off the dance floor.

We went to the table to sit with Larry and Lanna. I made the introductions for Jacob, but clearly Larry and Jacob had met earlier. I'd showed Larry pictures of Jacob, and Jacob pictures of Larry, so they had that connection. Jacob said we were going to step outside for a few, but we'd be right back.

He escorted me out of the club so we could hear each other talk. I knew I was going to get a lecture like a school girl. I deserved to have fun. I was already thinking of my defense when he put me up against the cold brick wall and kissed me like a lover. I was thrilled, and totally not expecting this response.

"Jenna, I'm sorry I was late, but I had a great meeting tonight and wanted to find you to celebrate. Thank you for not calling me every ten minutes to find out when I was leaving. I love that about you. I'm so glad that you know I'll be with you as soon as I can, always."

"Jacob, it's about respect. You tell me a certain time, and don't call to say how much later it's going to be, you wouldn't treat a business associate that way, but that's how you want to treat your own wife?"

I really enjoy Larry's company and he's very bright and funny. You didn't show up for dinner that was rude. I would never do that to you in front of your friends or family. I would never put you in that uncomfortable situation. Do you understand how you made me feel tonight? I'm not saying I'm not glad you are here, that Rick was a jerk, but there never would have been a Rick situation if you would have been a man of your word."

"You are harsh woman."

"Yeah, the truth fits that way sometimes, doesn't it? I've had a few drinks and you know what else, I think I'll go have a few more. If you are going to be in a bad mood, go home Jacob. If you want to have fun with me and my friends, then come on in and join the fun. I'm sure I won't have trouble finding a dance partner, so do what you want; I'm here to have fun and dance."

"Jenna,"

"No Jacob, no talk, just fun tonight. I deserve it, and frankly so do you! Let's hit the floor." We went to the table, ordered drinks and found our way out to the dance floor. Jacob was an impressive dancer, my man has moves.

We had so much fun together dancing, laughing and drinking all night. Jacob wouldn't let me drive home at closing time. He thought I'd been drinking too much, so we got a hotel room and had a delightful date night. He only really relaxes when he's away from home and work. I'm just now figuring this out about him. I wonder if he realizes this or not about himself.

"Good morning Jacob, what do you want to do today sweetheart?"

"What time is it?"

"According to this hotel clock, it's officially 9:47 a.m. Guess we slept in this morning. I'm starving, are you hungry?"

"We have to leave. We have a family reunion today out at my Grandma's house."

"I'm sorry, what did you just say? How long has this been planned and why are you just telling me now?"

"I didn't want you to stress over seeing everyone after the legal actions between our families. You are my wife, and they are going to have to accept you, because we are married now. This is sort of a welcome to the family get together."

"You couldn't tell me that before now? Don't you trust me to handle stress? You put me in a situation where I have no choice. I'm so mad at you right now. I drank like a fish last night knowing I could rest today, and now I have to be on best behavior for inspection and acceptance of your family. Thanks Jacob! (I was throwing on my clothes). Take me to my car!"

"Wait, (he was throwing his clothes on too, shoes in his and ran to catch up with me at the elevator). Jenna, you have to go."

"I will go because I would never treat you the way you have treated me, but you need to take me to my car so I can get home, shower and change before I have to be your show and tell. You can't keep treating me this way Jacob; I'm a person, not a possession!"

"Do you really feel that way?"

"Examine your actions, what do you think? Step back and look objectively at the facts, and then we'll have this discussion of what I should and shouldn't feel. Right now, I don't have the luxury of discussing my feelings and why not? Because I have to be all fake and smiles for your families impending inspection and judgments. Thanks for the ride Jacob, are you coming home for us to ride together to the reunion, or are we doing that separate too?"

CHAPTER 2

Family Reunion

Jacob followed me home and we both got in the shower to clean up. I couldn't look myself in the mirror for being so horrible to Jacob. I stopped and went to him. "Jacob, I'm sorry, I should have never said those things. I was being emotional and unkind to you, please forgive me."

"No, you were right, we really don't have time now for a needed conversation."

"Okay, I just wanted to say I'm sorry if I hurt you, I don't want to do that, that's all I have to say, I'll go." I noticed my voice getting quieter and quieter, so I knew that tears weren't far behind. "I'll be ready in about 10 minutes. Do we need to bring anything?"

"I took care of the food for you." I turned around and walked back down the hall to my bathroom, mumbling to myself out loud, of course he did, like everything he makes the decisions and I follow along, always as an afterthought. It gives me a sick feeling thinking about it. I can't go into the lion's den feeling this negative.

Standing in front of my bathroom mirror, I closed my eyes, leaned on the counter and prayed for strength, "God please help me be a good wife to my husband. I love that big idiot. Change me and him so we can be a better team together, amen." I opened my eyes, and I could see Jacob standing right behind me and he said "Amen!"

I didn't know he was right behind me, following me to my bathroom. Did he know I was about ready to cry? Did he know I was going to pray for God to help us? I could see my shocked face in the mirror and knew we didn't have time for a conversation. So I changed the subject quickly. I looked down at my brush.

"Am I dressed appropriately? What will the other women wear?"

"It's a casual deal, everyone will be in jeans." I had a black pair of jeans, with black knee high boots a red V-neck shirt and an animal print black white and silver oversized scarf around my neck. I checked my nails because I knew the women would want to see my ring. My nails looked great. I thought about bringing my camera, but thought I'd wait for the next family reunion so I'd know more what to expect.

"You look great, you always do."

"Thank you for saying that it means more than you will ever know to hear that from you."

"Are you ready to go?

"Sure, ready or not here we come."

"It's my family Jenna, they aren't that bad."

"Oh, I thought I was your family now, thanks for the clarification, I feel much better." I just pushed myself past him and walked to the truck. There it is again, that tickle in my lower throat that makes me feel sick to my stomach and makes me want to tear up all at the same time. Why can't I just keep my mouth shut? *(Jenna just shut up. This is his family all you need to do is be quiet and smile for a few hours. Just make it happen self, make it happen with a smile.)*

Jacob got in the truck and I turned on his radio and just started singing because I was working on getting my-self ready to see Ms. Ruth's farm house again. The last time I was there, she was alive. The last time I was there, Jacob and I were falling in love.

My Granny shot and killed his grandma. His family now owns my Granny and Partners land and house they'd owned next to each other for the last 50 years. This is going to be an emotional day, but I will not cry, no matter what, even if I break my ankle again. I will not show that I am human, that I have feelings and that they have the power to break me. I will be kind but distant, what else could they expect?

"Do you want to go and see your Grandmas old house, we will make the time if you want, do you?"

"Thanks for asking, but I can't do that today, I've promised myself no tears today, and I can't go there, not today. Is that okay with you?"

"Fine I just thought we are here if you wanted to, no pressure, not trying to control you."

"Not feeling defensive and pouty, are you?" I immediately threw my hand over my mouth in shock that I said that out loud, or that I even thought that. I just looked up at Jacob. "I am so sorry. I see you as a strong, loving intelligent man and that's my truth about you. I can never drink that much ever again I'm talking like a crazy woman."

"Every time you open your mouth, you are throwing spears at my heart. I know we need to have some conversations, and I have been listening to what you've said, intentionally or prayers to God, and I am not blind."

"Jacob, please don't say anything else, I can't walk in there crying, and if you say one more word, I swear to my God, I'm going to lose it." I had to turn my head and look out the window to regain my composure. No tears, breathe, no tears. We are here, I must be ready to spend time with my new family.

"Hold on and I'll walk around and open the door for you. You like that don't you?"

"Yes." Jacob got out walked around the back of the truck and opened my door. I was taking off my seatbelt and he held out his hand to help me out of the truck. Just one touch from him, and I felt so much better. I just smiled at him and apparently bit my bottom lip, because Jacob pulled me to him and kissed me like there was no one else around. Like I meant the world to him, and that I mattered.

I was so glad he was holding me because I didn't want to be anywhere else but in his arms. After intense kissing he realized his brothers were walking out to our truck, so he let me go and whispered in my ear, I love you.

"I love you too."

And with that, his brothers came up and said, "you two need a room?"

I just said "ha, ha "and we all walked up to the house together. Jacob reached out for my hand and in the other he carried in the pies. Then he said, "I'll go with you babe." I just smiled that he was showing me he was picking me over his brothers. He didn't have to do that, but this is my first encounter with his family since our wedding and I might need him close by my side. I just leaned over to kiss him.

He whispered back at me," do not bite that lip again."

I just smiled and whispered, "thanks for having my back".

The first hour or two went by non-eventful. They were nice but not overly friendly or welcoming. At some point I released my death grip off Jacob's hand, and he went to visit with his brothers and knocked down a few beers with them. The boys were playing football in the yard, and asked if I'd like to break a leg?

I hollered back, no thanks, I've already done that. They

all laughed. It's really sad to know I'll always be Jenna the klutz. Thank goodness I didn't have a cast on today. After the sun was going down, the men started playing poker. The women all played a card game called "tic" and the men gambled in the parlor room. The kids just sort of ran around inside and outside, being kids, laughing and having fun.

I had lots of great memories being out here and I was hoping that today and tonight was a first step toward loving me and accepting me as one of them. But I overheard the women whispering in the kitchen and realized I will always be the outsider. They were disappointed that Jacob had married beneath them.

I needed air so I walked out to the tree swing where I magically fell in love with Jacob. The kids were off chasing lightening bugs, so I got on the swing and started to swing and remembered better days between our families.

Just then I felt someone's hands on my bottom, pushing me in the swing. At first, I thought it was Jacob, who else would touch me on my rear on purpose? And then he spoke, "Jenna are you having fun today?"

It was Andrew, Jacobs's best friend and closest brother. I just said, "how about you Andrew, are you having fun? Is your girlfriend here today?"

"No, she had to work. She's a nurse and was called for a time and a half shift. She wants a big wedding, so that's where she is."

"Oh, are you two engaged?"

"Not yet, but she may be the one."

"Andrew stop pushing me please, I'm ready to get down."

"No, I don't think so; I think you are taking my brother for a ride, Jenna."

"Andrew, do not make me jump out of this swing, because you know I'll fall and break my ankle and you will be blamed." He stopped pushing me and by the time it slowed down enough I jumped out of it. Jacob was by my side.

"Andrew we should eat something to wash down all the beers we've had today." I took Jacob's hand and we started walking to the house for some food, because I was starving, and the food everyone brought looked delicious. There was food out most of the day for kids and family to eat at will, but dinner was everyone eating together. I felt bad that I didn't get to cook anything for his family.

Andrew waited until we were all inside before he announced his thoughts in a booming volume for everyone to hear, "what's wrong Jacob? Jenna can cook in the bedroom but not in the kitchen?"

Jacob just squeezed my hand and said, "Why Andrew, what makes you think she can't cook in the kitchen?"

"Okay then, what did you bring, I want to try it?" And before I could open my mouth Jacob said,

"We brought three pies, one cherry and two apples. What did you bring?"

"I grilled the ribs they are really good did you get some? I got one of those green ceramic eggs and this was my first attempt with the meat and it was so juicy I couldn't believe it. You need to get some and try it; it melts in your mouth, falls off the bone it's that tender."

Just like that, the brothers were off talking about something else, and I was off the hook. Jacob was there defending me to his family. He's smart and wasn't overly protective or controlling but was my safety net the whole day.

It was almost midnight, and I had a terrible headache and I just wanted to go home, to sleep in my own bed. The boys were getting louder and louder and the women were worn out chasing after their kids and cleaning the messes that didn't stop.

Then I saw a guitar in the corner of the room and without thinking, I picked it up and moved out on the porch to a straight back chair by myself and started tuning it.

Then I began picking a tune I remembered from long ago, called the Red River Valley, my dad used to like that old western song. It wasn't easy to play with my artificial nails, but I was getting the hang of it. When I looked up, Jacob was leaning on the door post across from me.

"Please don't stop playing, that was beautiful. I didn't know you could play. My Grandpa used to play that guitar and we finally have someone who can make it sing like he did. Do you know any other songs?"

I just smiled, he walked over and kissed me on the forehead, and I started playing "Will the circle be unbroken, by and by Lord, by and by, there's a better home a waiting, in the sky Lord, in the sky". Then I played Amazing Grace, and when I looked up, Jacob's dad was leaning on the door post staring at me, and several of the brothers and lots of kids (from the girlfriends) all staring at me in silence. I felt self-conscience playing Jacob's Grandpas' guitar so after the song was over, I thanked them for letting me play such a beautiful instrument and stood up to take it back inside the house.

I asked Jacob's dad if he played, and he said, "not as well as you, but if you want, maybe we could play something together"? Then he pulled a harmonica out of his pocket. That was the first gesture of accepting me he had expressed, and I just reached up and hugged him. He hugged me back in sort of a surprised hug fashion. I sat back down and even though my fingers were sore and killing me, I didn't say a word.

One of the brothers got his violin out of its case and we started bonding with a mutual love of music. The little kids were dancing out in the grass and catching fire flies, couples were dancing on the porch, the teenage girls were singing and my first family reunion was ending on a sweet note, literally.

It was almost 1:00 a.m. in the morning and kids were either sleeping all over the house or they were crying, tired wanting to go home to bed. We were tired too. Jacob made our excuses, and we were finally leaving. He reached to take my hand but my fingers hurt so bad from playing the guitar that I winced. Jacob stared right through me and quickly let go of my hand until we got out to our truck. Then when he opened the door and the light came on in the truck he grabbed my hand hard and pulled them up to examine them. "Jenna, why did you do this to yourself? Two of your fingers are actually bleeding."

"I did it for you Jacob, for your family. I enjoyed seeing them smile and join in together like my family does when we get together and sing. It was my comfort zone and I was just out of practice. I would do it again if I got a hug from your dad again. That was so sweet of him. There is always a cost to be paid for relationships; it's just that people usually don't see those sacrifices made for the benefit of others. I enjoyed making music with your dad and brothers."

"You are a beautiful person, you really are. I appreciate you and I know I do a horrible job showing you. I love you my little accident prone Jenna. Thank you for bringing music back to my family. We haven't had such a great time together since Grandpa died and I was a teenage boy. Thank you for being my family, you held your own today, and that took some work with all my brothers.

You were right about what you said earlier too, on all of it. I'm stubborn and it takes me a while to be as honest and open as you are with me. I love our relationship and I know I need to do better for us, just don't give up on me."

"Not ever, we are forever, start believing that, believing in us. We are a sure thing, you should bet on us, we are all in both of us till death. Start acting like you believe it. I'm not one of your temporary girl friends that just requires dinner and sex, I want all of you.

I want the pillow talk, I want the phone calls just because you love me. I want the flowers every now and then, I want the romance. I want the relationship, the whole package. I can be patient, but you've got to show me you want the same things. I don't want your things Jacob, I just want you, I want you and me, quality time together, I want us time."

"I want that too. I want you more every day and I'm shocked that that's even possible. I always thought I was shallow, just a sex junkie, but you captured me, I don't know how you do it, but I'm lost in you."

"I don't want you to feel lost, because I draw my strength and security from you. We are a team. We just need to work on our verbal communication skills. We may make each other furious, but we have the security to know we can cool down and discuss matters in an adult fashion. We know that no matter what, we are solid."

CHAPTER 3

Picture Perfect

Jacob and I started spending more quality time together after our heart to heart talk. I had noticed big improvements with him being considerate of my time and my feelings. When he was running later than planned, which was still all the time, but now he would call me to let me know a more accurate time.

I adore him, he's a guy and what guy ever gets it right without a woman's help? Really? My job as the dutiful and loving wife is not to be a nag, but to just tell him how I feel and what I'm going through. His actions and responses are all on him. And so far he's done a wonderful job of meeting my needs and wants. I am much happier now that I have more time with my husband on a more frequent basis.

Jacob was making plans to finalize a big deal in China, and was going to be gone a week, possibly two. He hired an interpreter, and he and another business associate were headed to China. He asked me to go with him, but I have no desire to visit China, especially when he would be working around the clock.

I don't speak the language, and right now is a busy time for my photography classes. I don't want to miss anything. I'm pretty sure Jacob was somewhat relieved to know he didn't need to worry about me in a distant land. He could just focus on his work and know I was home safe and sound. That was fine with me. I would miss him, but it would only be a few days, a week, two tops.

Jacob set up our Skype and Zoom accounts on my laptops so we could see each other over the miles even though we couldn't be in the same room together. He wasn't sure which would get better reception, so he set up two different ways for us to be able to see and hear each other while he was gone.

Knowing that he was going to be gone for a while, I bought a red-hot lover outfit that came with a small red leather whip. I put on my nightie with red high heel pump, makeup on, and hair long and full when Jacob Skyped me for the first time. I was trying to make him miss me while he was away.

Well, his business partner was in the room with him at the time of our first Skype, and Jacob was trying to cover the screen, with me in my sexy red-hot lover outfit. I was trying to hide my body when I saw his business partner's mouth drop to the floor. Clearly it didn't have the desired results I was wanting from Jacob. I was totally embarrassed, and hung up our connection. Jacob called me immediately after my Skype fiasco.

"Jenna, it's the middle of the day here when its night there, I'm at work here darling. You can't wear that kind of attire on Skype. But I want you to keep that outfit for when I get home, you are sexier than hell in that, and that whip you can't do that to me long distance. I'm going to have to buy a hooker over here to release my energy."

"Very funny Jacob, but no hooker, street walker, girlfriend, you are off the market, unless we have an open relationship. After all I do have this outfit and would like to break it in."

"No, no open relationship, you aren't dating anyone, and I'm not either, but seriously Jenna, keep your clothes on while I'm away. Can you do that? And Skype knowing that I'm at work and others could be in the room."

"Well, now that I know the rules, I will try to keep things sweet and innocent, for you long distance, just know when you get home, my red trampy outfit is waiting for you."

"Oh, I won't forget that, and I don't think my business associate will ever look at you the same way again. You may never get to speak to him again. He's been married several years, and his wife isn't as how shall I say it, openly adventurous as you are."

"I don't even want to know how you would know that. Men talk way more than women do about stuff they should keep private."

"No babe not me, but most men just have vivid imaginations you know a picture is worth a thousand words and that's all I'm going to say. Jenna, you need to eat while I'm gone. You look like you've lost weight and I've only been gone five days."

I was glad he couldn't see my face, because I really hadn't been hungry since he left. I just smiled and said, "no problem, I'll eat more."

"Before you get back to work, your brother Andrew called me last night, and told me he was supposed to keep an eye on me while you are gone. He wants to take me to town for dinner and dancing. Are you okay with this, or is he just making up stuff? "

"No, I did tell him to keep a watchful eye, but I didn't tell him to take you out on a date when I'm thousands of miles away. If he doesn't drink, you'll be fine, but if he drinks, you do not ride home with him, no matter what, you promise me, or I'm coming home now."

"I didn't tell you this to upset you, I'm just touching base and communicating with you. I won't ride with him if he drinks."

"I love you, but my meeting starts in a few minutes, and I need to get my business partner oxygen so he can come back to life after your Skype show. Love you babe. Be good and keep your clothes on!"

"Bye Jacob, I love you too."

I called Andrew, "Hey Andrew this is your sister-in-law, and I talked it over with Jacob, he said if you want to go out for dinner and dancing, that would be fine, but only under one condition.

"Jenna we are family, we don't do conditions."

"Then I'm not going."

"Okay wait, let me hear it, what's the condition?"

"No drinking."

"What if I get thirsty, or choke on my food?"

"You know what I mean Andrew, no alcohol."

"Jenna, you need to chill out and be reasonable. I'll meet you in the middle, and I won't get drunk. How about that?"

"Do you promise not to get drunk Andrew, not even tipsy?"

"You act like I have a drinking problem."

"No, I just know that I love my husband, and he's out of the country. I don't want you acting in a way that would cause hurt to you and your relationship with Jacob."

"Don't flatter yourself, you are cute, but you're not all that."

"Actually Andrew, I am all that, but that's beside the point. If you promise to behave, and we go out as brother and sister to have a fun night together out on the town, then I'd love to go. What day are we going?"

"How about Friday night?"

"Sure, what time?"

"How about I pick you up at 6:00 and we can eat around 6:45. I'll call and get reservations. Edward and his girlfriend want to come too if you are alright with that."

"Sure, the more Jamison's the merrier."

I tried on a couple of outfits but decided on an attractive tight cream-colored dress with a thin black belt above my waist and my black patent leather two-inch heels. I pulled my hair up and let it hang down in ringlets in the back and just around my face. I had black onyx earrings that were rectangle in shape to match the black bra part on the top of my beige dress.

The top looked like a dressy black bra, and the rest of my short dress was sort of spandex material that was very form fitting, and it was a soft beige/peach color on the back of the dress and beige/peach on the front up to the waist then the breast area was sequenced black with a small thin black belt below the bra line. It doesn't sound that cute, but it was stunning on if I do say so myself.

Andrew came to the door and when I opened it, he said, "Jenna, I'm going to need back up to beat the guys off you tonight."

I just smiled and gave him a peck on the cheek. "Thanks for saying that Andrew. You clean up nice too."

I assumed that since I was going to dinner with the Jamison brothers that we'd be going to one of the popular steak houses in the area. But the night was not going to go as I expected. We went to a Japanese Steak House.

The chief, if that's what you call him, cut, chopped, sliced and diced things in front of us and pretty much threw the food on our plates in front of us. It was semi-entertaining but the man cutting and chopping our food was very sloppy and kept staring at me. I was thinking maybe I should have worn jeans and a sweatshirt because this man actually has sharp knives and likes to throw things.

At one point, he asked me to open my mouth because he wanted to throw a shrimp into my mouth. I shook my head no and felt even more uncomfortable. The food was okay, but I'd never go there again.

After dinner, my brother-in -law Eddie, and his girlfriend Kim joined us at the club. My friends Larry and Lanna were in town, so I asked the Jamison brothers if they minded if I invited a couple to join us. They were fine with that. We reached the club and again, the bouncer let me in for free. I have got to learn his name he's so good to me.

Andrew, Eddie and Kim came in after me. I reached Larry on the phone in case he and Lanna were free, I told him I would love it if they could join us. They had a different band tonight, but the band had a rocking beat, and they had a great sound, it was enjoyable.

I danced with steady Eddie for a while. I really enjoyed laughing and talking with him. Andrew was a watchdog all night long. Andrew didn't like to dance, but I did notice he wasn't without a drink in his hand. He took his brotherly duties very seriously. Later in the night Larry showed up. Lanna wasn't feeling well, but after he got her dinner, she just wanted to sleep, so he thought he'd come by and kick back a few with me and my brothers.

I introduced him to Andrew and Eddie and Kim, and then Larry and I hit the dance floor. What I didn't realize at that time was that by the time Larry and I got from our seats to the dance floor, the fast song was over and a slow one started. Larry was polite and asked if I wanted to sit out, dance or just talk. It seemed harmless, so I said we could dance to a slow song. I mean really, Jacob has two brothers watching over me, what harm could come from this?

Unfortunately, Andrew had been drinking and thought that it would be funny to take a picture of me and Larry slow dancing together and send it to Jacob. I had no idea at the time, that he did this. Larry and I were out on the floor talking and laughing and having a great time.

Chapter 4

My Brother's Keeper

We came back to the table and Eddie met me before we reached our table and said, "Jenna I'm so sorry, I didn't know Andrew was going to do that."

"Do what?" I got to the table, and Andrew had the phone to his ear and was covering the other ear to hear. Then he pointed to me and motioned me to come here. Andrew just shook his head and said, "he has no sense of humor."

"Who?"

"Jacob, he's on the phone and wants to talk to you now."

I couldn't hear him, so I moved outside quickly because I knew with the time difference it was not a good time for him to be talking to me. Eddie stood in the doorway of the club so he could see and probably hear the conversation too. I finally got outside where I could talk to Jacob. He was furious that I was wearing underwear out in public, "it's flesh colored Jenna, like you are out there naked."

"No, it isn't, there is black all over the front of the dress."

"From the back it leaves nothing to the imagination. You were hanging all over Larry."

"Wait a minute, how do you know what I'm wearing and why do you think I'm acting like a slut? Jacob I'm with your brothers, don't be this way, I told you we were going to eat and dance. I'm not being vulgar by any stretch of the word."

"Andrew sent me a video of you bumping and grinding on the dance floor. I just turned and looked at Eddie, shaking my head and tears running down my face. He was yelling at me, when he stopped yelling, I took a deep breath.

"Sorry to hurt you Jacob. I never intentionally do or say anything that would hurt you or distract you from your important business. I don't know why Andrew sent you that video, or pictures I don't know why, but I'm sorry I hurt you."

He didn't say he loved me, he just yelled "Jenna I told you to keep your clothes on, and you are out in public practically naked." He slammed down the phone.

I just handed Eddie the phone and curled up on the ground outside on the pavement. Eddie picked me up and walked me to his car. I asked him if he would take me home. He said sure, let me get my date. I also asked him to tell Larry I was sorry I had to leave earlier than I had planned but thank him for my dance."

"What about Andrew?" I have nothing to say to him, but you can tell him anything you want. Eddie came out to the car and they were all with him, Larry, Andrew and Kim. Andrew came to my side of the car, and said, "Jenna don't make this a big deal, it was a joke, lighten up."

Andrew you hurt Jacob by your actions tonight, and I can't fix it with him half a world away. Your actions affect others Andrew, grow up!"

"Well, you know how you can fix the problem then, don't dress and act like a slut." Eddie can we please go home now, please just get me out of here?"

"Larry said he'd take you home Jenna, if you'd rather?"

"Larry thanks for the offer, but I should have driven and not trusted Andrew to be responsible for me or anyone else for that matter. I'll call you later this week." Edward started the car, and Andrew was still standing by my window. He said, "what Sis, no kiss goodbye?" Thank God Eddie just drove off. I was kind of hoping he would run over his feet, but that would have been unkind. But I still thought it.

I didn't want to cry I just wanted to have a fun evening and look what's happened. Eddie, I'm so sorry to intrude on a lovely night with you and Kim. Thank you for being trustworthy and giving me a ride home, I really appreciate it.

"Don't worry about Jacob, he will calm down. I'll call him in a few hours and tell him what really happened, that Andrew was just being an ass, and this whole thing got blown out of proportion."

"Thank you, Eddie, but I couldn't ask you to do that for me."

"You didn't ask me to and that's why I offered. Andrew was out of line, and Jacob just overreacted to his wife swaying with another man."

"Larry is a kid, a fun friend. He's sweet and has a girlfriend and Jacob knows him and has met Lanna his girlfriend too. I can't win with him no matter what I do. I keep trying to prove I'm trustworthy to my own husband, but it's never enough. Not even going out with two of his own brothers as watch dogs, no offense Eddie.

Thank you again for the ride home, sorry to dampen the mood for your evening. I hope you two can forget all this drama and just enjoy the rest of your evening together. Thanks again for the ride home."

"This will blow over, don't worry about it. Thanks again and goodbye." I knew I couldn't trust Andrew. Then there was that tickle in the back of my throat and all I could do was cry.

Jacob called me six different times and I didn't answer the phone. I couldn't. Eddie came over about 5:00 p.m. the next day to check on me. He said Jacob was sorry and couldn't get ahold of you. He thought maybe you lost your phone last night. But I see your phone on the table. Jenna he's furious with Andrew but not you.

"Eddie, his words were so unkind to me on the phone."

"Jenna, are you going somewhere? You have luggage by the door."

"He will never trust me. I've tried everything I know and still after all this time together he will not trust me. I can't spend my life with someone who can't believe in me. I've done nothing but love and support him the best I know how, but he can't keep treating me this way.

If he wants me gone, he doesn't have to leave the country, I'll leave his country. I still have my house in Missouri, I have no choice. I'm going to stay at a hotel or an apartment until my photography classes are over, and then I'll be out of Kentucky for good. I love you brother, I will always wish you and your family the best, always."

"Jenna, please do not ask me to tell my brother that you are leaving him. He will always associate you leaving with me and I couldn't bear that burden. Don't do this to me. Jenna please, talk to him, answer your phone."

"I'm sorry Eddie, I shouldn't have said anything to you. Please ignore the ranting's of a heart broken woman. I will talk to Jacob, don't worry, I won't put you in that position with your brother." The phone rang and I went to the phone.

"Jenna, thank God, did you lose your phone?"

"No."

"Did you know I was calling you and you just didn't

answer?"

"Yes."

"Mature Jenna, really mature."

"Did you call six times to call me names again? I think I got your message loud and clear last night. Is that all Jacob?"

"Jenna, no wait, Edward called me and told me what an ass Andrew was, and how things were not as they were presented to me. I over-reacted and I'm sorry. I've been sick with worry about you. I couldn't do any business today, I had to hear your voice."

"Okay well you've heard my voice so hopefully you will be able to make your business dealings for the rest of the day. Will that be all?"

"Don't be cold to me, I can't live with that."

"Jacob, what do you want from me? I've given you my heart and soul, been nothing but honest with you, yet it's never enough. I'm not enough for you Jacob, and I can't live with a man who doesn't know me enough to trust me, not again. I wanted your love and trust more than you will ever know. But I don't know what else I could possibly do or say to convince you that I love you and I'm faithful.

How stupid do you think I am? That I would go out with two of your brothers and act in an inappropriate way? It's like you don't even know me. I thought you knew me better than anyone, but we are back to this same song and dance. You don't know me at all. You broke my heart not just with your unkind words, but by your lack of trust. Without trust, we have nothing."

"Jenna don't talk like this! I will die without you. I love you, I'm an idiot. I was a fool, but please don't destroy me. Don't leave me Jenna." He as crying so hard I couldn't understand him.

"Jacob, stop, I'll stay until you get back. When are you coming back?"

"I will call you tonight with the day and time. Jenna,

thank you for waiting so we can talk this out and I'm sorry. I love you and please forgive me. I will make this right, I'm so sorry."

"Goodbye Jacob."

"Jenna please don't say goodbye, not to me, say see you later, anything but goodbye."

"Best Wishes, Jacob." Click.

Jenna, Jenna, I've lost her. I'm a world away, and I've lost my reason for living, what did I just do? What am I going to do?

I had forgotten that Eddie was getting me a cup of coffee when I answered Jacob's call. He came into the room, and I was once again curled up into a ball.

"Jenna, are you okay?"

"No Eddie, I will never be okay again." I didn't know it, but Jacob had left his business associate in China to finalize the deal on his own and he caught a flight non-stop back to the states. By the time I stopped crying, spent the day taking pictures of a house that I was leaving, of the beautiful Kentucky land I was leaving, of the horses I was leaving, I took my photographs to my photo studio to develop them. I printed the prints and hung them to dry. Sort of symbolic, I felt hung out to dry. I was almost ready for bed and I heard a knock on the door. I went to the door, it was Andrew.

"Jenna, its Andrew, let me in."

"No Andrew, I will not! This is still my home for the next few hours anyway, and I will not let you inside. Not when I don't have witnesses."

"Then just listen to me, through the door. I am so sorry, Jenna. I didn't mean it, I swear it. I think Jacob is going to kill himself, I've never heard him this way, never Jenna. I'm so sorry. Please don't leave him. This is entirely my fault and I know it. If you go, he will never forgive me. I screwed up, I do that a lot, but don't destroy him because of me. I am begging you Jenna, don't leave him. I'll do anything, just name it, anything please Jenna, please!"

Andrew was crying, pounding on the door. I could see him from the living room window, and he looked pathetic. These stupid men don't get that their actions have consequences.

"Andrew, stop it! You've made your choices and created this nightmare that we are all in the aftermath. Andrew you are a self-centered, immature boy. Your poor choices have negatively impacted my life. Destroying a couple that honestly loved one another, and I will miss him every day of my life. But I will hate your behavior forever. You will reap what you've sown."

"Jenna, if I kill myself, will this right my wrong?" I saw a gun in his hand, and I ran to unlock the door.

"Andrew if you pull that trigger, I will have to kill myself too, then Jacob will have to kill himself and your dad and brothers. NO ONE is killing himself or herself! Do you hear me Andrew? Give me the gun! Hand it to me right now! You said you'd do anything, well, hand me the gun right now, Andrew in my hand, now!"

Andrew handed me the gun. Eddie came up from around the back of the house and tackled him to the ground. I'd never seen steady Eddie upset before, and he was inconsolable. I didn't even know Eddie was at the house.

"Andrew what the hell are you thinking? You need help, professional mental help. You can't threaten to take your life ever again. You brought a gun to Jenna's. That's not an option. We love you, you stupid F'ing idiot. We love you. Keep it together Andrew."

I took the gun and calmly walked into the house and locked the brothers outside the house. Then they both ran to the front door pounding and yelling. Jenna, don't do it, don't do it!

I went to the window and said in a calm tone, "I have no intention of killing anything or anyone. I was just keeping the crazy out and away from me. Now if you two don't mind, please just go home. Leave me alone, please leave me alone.

Jacob loves you both, you are family, and I will always wish you both the best. Andrew I will forgive you one day, I'm sorry for what I said to you just now, it was unkind and hurtful. Please just go away now!"

"Jenna I'm so sorry, but please forgive Jacob."

"Eddie, please take Andrew somewhere to get him professional help immediately. He seriously needs an intervention now." I carried the gun and went up stairs to the master bathroom. I emptied all the bullets out of the gun and threw the bullets into the trash can, laid the gun on the counter, because I wasn't sure how to dispose of someone's gun.

I started a hot bubble bath and set my body in the Jacuzzi. I didn't take off my clothes for fear that another one of Jacob's brother would come in and I would be naked. I did take off my shoes, but I just slipped out of my jeans and left my bra and undies on as I got into the tub. The hot water was relaxing and after all the drama I'd dealt with around and concerning Andrew, I more than ever wanted to get away, far away.

I had to say goodbye to the love of my life forever. Why didn't he trust me? Why did he think I was a slut? Why would he believe Eddie when he talked to him, but not me when he's supposed to know me better than anyone?

Long after the water was cold, I let most the water out and refilled it with hot water and bubbles again. This time I took my wet underwear off and sat in the hot water. I couldn't get out of the tub even if I wanted to, I felt like a wet noodle. The water was cold again for a second time and all I had to do was get out. I drained the water and pulled myself out of the deep tub.

As I stood up to get a towel, in the mirror I saw him in the reflection, Jacob. I immediately fell to my knees. He ran to me, he looked horrible, worse than horrible. He looked like I felt. I was wet, cold and naked and I couldn't believe Jacob was here. Then he said my name, "Jenna," it was his voice, but unsteady and heart sick.

"Jenna my love, I'm a fool and I'm so sorry I was unkind to you on the phone. I was a world away from you and I was so hateful, so vicious. I was just missing you and jealous because I couldn't be the one holding you in my arms, and I never believed for one minute you would break our trust. I know I can trust you. You are not the problem, I am.

I'm jealous and I try not to be controlling but I'm flawed. I love you and need you and if you leave me, I will be lost to myself forever. Do you still love me?" I couldn't look at him in his condition and not be honest with him. "Jenna, tell me do you love me?"

I couldn't hold him in suspense, he sounded so desperate. I said the only truth I knew, "Yes Jacob, I love you, if I didn't it wouldn't hurt so bad when you..."

"You said yes, you still love me?"

"Yes Jacob, I love you."

"Are you leaving me? Have I ruined my life forever, our lives forever?"

"I should go Jacob, but I don't know if I have the strength to leave you."

"I love you and I promise you I will never, ever, ever hurt you that way again. I will do whatever you want me to do to make this right. I'm so sorry. Jenna, I'm sorry! I dropped everything a half a world away to be with you and tell you I love you. I'm broken hearted that I did this to you and me. I'm sorry what do I do to fix this?"

"I'm freezing on this cold floor. Help me so I can stand up." He quickly grabbed my arms and lifted me up. I was helpless once I was in his arms. He just hugged me so tight I didn't think, I could breathe. I didn't care I could die here and be happy. Jacob was lifting me up to carry me to the bed and he saw the gun on the counter.

"What are you doing with a gun? You weren't going to kill yourself because of me, were you? You can't do that ever."

"No Jacob, you've got it all wrong, it was Andrew's gun. He came over with it earlier and threatened to kill himself in front of me. Eddie was here and I got the gun away from him. Eddie was taking Andrew to the hospital for professional help."

Jacob just squeezed me and wrapped me under the sheets in our bed. I missed him, his feel, his smell, his strength. I didn't want things to be different between us, but he keeps ripping my heart out. He kissed me and I needed him. I was shivering. I felt his warmth, his strength, his spirit with me. I needed him as desperately as he needed me. We belonged to each other. Jacob was ferocious toward me, in need of me but holding back. "Jacob, what is it?"

"I love you so much, I seriously considered killing myself if I couldn't get you to forgive me. I couldn't live without you. I would be an empty shell. You are my life, and I am so sorry. I'm afraid to be myself with you because I screw things up and I don't want you to leave me. I just have to be careful. I can never hurt you again, because you'll leave me. I can't be myself because I am not good enough for you. I don't deserve you and I have to change. I can change, Jenna, just give me another chance, please!"

"Jacob, stop it! You have to stop talking this desperate life changing talk. I married you because I loved you! I don't want you to be someone else, someone you're not. Do we need to work on your communication skills and trusting me? Yes, big problem areas!

It was your stupid brother being silly, sending a picture or video and with the time difference and our loneliness from being apart, things got misunderstood. I need you to be you. All you! I need you to take me and want me. I can't stand you holding back anything from me ever.

Whatever happens between us Jacob, we need be true and honest with ourselves and to each other. If you love me Jacob, you need to trust me 100%. We are not going to be dishonest with one another. Not in our bed, not in our home, not now, not ever Jacob. Honesty remember the deal breaker!"

He grabbed me, threw me under him and we were like a pair of wild animals, desperate for one another. I almost lost the man of my dreams, the man who held my heart and my soul. I would do anything for this man. And I could see from the pain in his eyes he really loved me greatly too. Why does he have to be so hurtful if he loves me, why would he continue this bad behavior with me? At least he's willing to admit when he's wrong, and say he's sorry.

I keep thinking if I had told Andrew no to dinner, none of this would have happened, and you would have your big business deal, and my world wouldn't have come crashing down. Do you not know how much I love you after all this time? I'm your wife."

"I know, I'm just an insecure fool and I'm so sorry for being an unkind husband to you. I'm so sorry; please forgive me, say you forgive me baby. Tell me you forgive me. I need to hear you say those words to me. You need to say it to me and mean it."

"I do forgive you. I always will forgive you because that's what people do who love each other. We make mistakes and we forgive. I can't lose you because I can't exist without you either. I was hurt and wanted to leave the hurt behind, but that would mean I would have to leave the man that holds my heart and soul. I can't live without my heart, without my soul."

"You amaze me over and over. We will be a stronger couple after we move on from this stupidity, I brought on us. Let's just go away from here. Away from my family and my work where do you want to go? Where can I take you?"

"I don't need anything or any place, just you, only you. I don't want to go anywhere. I don't need to run away from home. We are home. I won't be run off from my home, our home, by one idiot brother. I don't think he was trying to be malicious he just made a cruel choice and your reaction set things in a downward spiral."

"Jenna..."

He said my name in his tone and inflections that was my Jacob, he spoke my name with the tenderness the strength, the passion, he's back, he's revived, and he's here with me. We are a living strength for one another. I smiled.

"Are you hungry?"

"Yes, I'm so hungry I'm about ready to pass out."

"Do we have any food in the house?"

"I don't even know."

"I'll go grab something and bring it up to you."

He threw on his jeans and ran down stairs and he was back in 10 minutes. I went to the bathroom and was crying. I think I was just so happy to have him back that my body just had to release all this pressure, pain, joy. I was just washing off my face and coming back to the bed and Jacob saw my face. I wish I could cry like some of those women on television who cry so pretty and graceful, but no I have the big red face, swollen eyes, runny nose the whole ugly thing.

"You're crying what is it? Are you sick?"

"No, I'm just hungry, emotionally drained and I'm just so happy you are finally here. I missed you and two weeks away from each other was too long."

"Come here and eat something. We have Diet Dr. Pepper, cheese and crackers, peanut butter and jelly sandwiches and two large glasses of milk." We had our protein fix. After my stomach was satisfied, I was ready for a nap, I was physically and emotionally exhausted.

"Do you think you should call and check on your

brother or your business partner? I'm sure Andrew will be better if he knows you don't hate him, and then he will be able to move on from this nightmare too."

"Sure, that's so you, thinking of others, my brother and my business. Yes, I'll make those calls, but you are my priority. I love you honey."

"I love you too."

Chapter 5

Opportunity Knocks

Jacob and I were in-separable for weeks on end after our China incident. We appreciated one another and respected what we had together now more than ever. I've told him I forgave him and that things were good between us many times, but I think he still feels like he owes me for putting us through all the drama. He really hasn't let me out of his sight since he thought I was leaving him. I don't think he or I have ever been so rattled to our very core like we were at the thought of almost losing each other.

Edward took Andrew to a psych ward for evaluation after he threatened to kill himself and come to find out, Andrew did have a problem, a secret drinking problem that he'd been fighting since high school. He was now acknowledging his problems and is attending AA meetings to get healthy.

He has been clean for a week. He asked Jacob and me to forgive him and Jacob had already called him and told him all was forgiven. I couldn't lie to him, I told him I forgave him, but that it would take a lot of time and lots of Christmas presents for years to come, to truly forget. Andrew is a sweet guy sober and I'm really glad he's getting his life together for a healthy future. His eyes and skin color even look healthier. I'm so happy for his progress.

My friend Larry broke up with Lanna. But after the dance floor fiasco, he was leery to spend time with me without Jacob going full scale crazy on me and him. I told him all was well and to let me worry about my husband. I can have friends of the opposite sex if I want to. I will have any friend I want. I've always had best friends that were guys. Maybe that's growing up an only girl in an extended family of all boys my age, I don't know. But I always seemed to have more fun with boys than girls.

That's not to say I don't have exceptional girlfriends, I do. But most of my friends were guys. The problem with that is when the guy grows up, you are still a friend, but with girlfriends and wives, that friendship is pretty much a distant memory.

I had skipped an entire week of photography classes. I was really behind in my photography lab hours, group work and research projects. In the meantime, Jacob won the account that he and Fred went to China to secure. The head of the China business account was impressed that Jacob would stop at nothing to, as he put it, "secure what was his at any price."

With Fred and Jacob's groundwork, they established a good working relationship, and the deal is finalized. Now Jacob has that pressure off his shoulders, and he's got about ten other situations that he has in the works. He really is a great businessman, and I haven't worked for an income, since I got married.

Jacob has never complained about me and money, ever. He had his checking accounts made into ours and his credit cards got my own cards on his accounts. He pays all the bills. I'm not a big kshopper but I don't think he would care if I was. He works hard for us and I respect that and try not to spend what isn't necessary. I splurge every once in a while on a thing or two, but it's the exception not the rule.

Jacob isn't traveling for his job for a while, but he's got people who have abilities that can take up some of the responsibilities he has been carrying by himself. I hate that Jacob and I almost crashed and burned, but good things have come out of it. Andrew is getting the help he needs, and Jacob is letting his leaders and business associates take on more responsibilities allowing him more free time with me.

It's his business he should have the freedom to choose what and when he works. He is really smart, and his mind is always thinking three or more steps ahead of me. I'm more laid back and he's full speed ahead all the time. We make a great team.

I really wanted to finish my photography courses. Jacob was supportive and would have done whatever he could to help me catch up from being behind. I worked really hard and enjoyed every minute of my work. For my mid-term I had to present a photo exhibit like I was presenting my work at the New York Art Institute.

I took my best pictures and saw a theme of nature, things and people that tell the story of enjoying the simple things. I printed out life size prints down to 60" prints. I was so glad that Jacob built and purchased my photo studio. It gave me the tools to learn and grow exponentially from just where I was a year ago, when I seriously started working with my photography.

I turned in my prints for the mid-term grade. My

instructor called me the next day and wanted to schedule a meeting to discuss my work. I said sure and talked to him after class. My instructor told me I got an "A" for my mid-term project and had some suggestions and good news.

"Thanks for meeting with me. The reason for this meeting is that I have a friend at the New York Art Institute, he called to say they had a presenter unexpectedly pull her work for the show that's this weekend. He asked if I had anything I could present. I think your mid-term prints would fit with their gallery event. I sent a copy of your prints for him to approve and they would like to invite you to present your work this weekend. This is a once in a lifetime opportunity.

You have talent and an eye for a different perspective of the everyday views. He needs to know your answer in the next three hours. You would have to get out there with your work Thursday by noon to the gallery. They will help you, or I could fly out and help you set up your work and lighting for the Friday night opening.

You need to be there for the Friday night's unveiling, and usually new artists are there for the Saturday's viewing too. It's an amazing opportunity to have your work showcased. Jenna, do you want this exposure? Are you interested in this once in a life time opportunity? Jenna?"

"Sorry, I think I'm in shock. Yes, I'm very interested this is an exciting opportunity for me and thank you for recommending me. My only concern is my husband and if he will think this is a good thing for me or not."

"This is your choice, you need to decide and let me know in the next few hours."

"Professor, you said I have a few hours to think this over, at least let me call my husband, do you mind if I have a few minutes? Is there somewhere I can go to speak privately?"

"Feel free to make your call here in my office, and I'm going to run down to the main lobby and grab a coffee.

You want one?"

"Yes please, with two creams, thank you." He turned and headed down the hall and I immediately called Jacob.

It was Monday almost 3:30 and he needed to know an answer by 6:00 our time to tell the gallery. I called Jacob in the middle of the day, which he knows I never do when he's at work, so he took my call.

"Jenna, are you okay?"

"Yes, but I need to talk to you as soon as you have a minute."

"Hold on,"

"Gentlemen I need to take this call, excuse me." I heard Jacob walking with his boots clonking on his work wooden floors. "Okay Jenna, you have my undivided attention, what is it?"

"First of all, thank you for that, for making me feel like a priority and not an interruption. And now the reason for my call. My professor thinks my photographs are good and he sent copies of my work to the New York Art Museum Gallery for an exhibit this weekend. They need an answer in the next hour or so.

My professor offered to come with me to help me set-up the exhibit. Do you think there is any way you could get off work on such short notice, to go with me to New York this week? I don't know what your work schedule looks like. I could even go out early and you could come out for the actual exhibit on Friday night, or I could just pass on this and feel good that my instructor thought my work is quality, and worthy of an exhibit. What do you think?"

"Baby, this is great news, I'm so happy for you. I want to be with you every step of the way. I can help haul, and carry things, whatever. Maybe we could take a couple of extra days there and go to some shows on Broadway, what do you think?"

"I think I need to tell my instructor we are doing this. Do you know if I need special insurance to fly my artwork with us to New York?"

"When do you want to leave?"

"He said I had to be there Thursday, by noon at the gallery."

"Okay, how about we fly out Wednesday. We can get a hotel close to the gallery and we will be more relaxed to enjoy this experience. I'll get my secretary on making those arrangements."

"Thank you, Jacob. I'm so excited!"

"We can pack and talk when I get home."

"Thanks, I won't keep you any longer."

"As always, I'm very proud of you and can't wait to share this experience with you."

"Thanks sweetheart, see you tonight."

My professor knocked at the door with his foot because his hands were full of coffee and I said come in, like it was my office. I was all smiles.

"I'm guessing by your smile that your answer is yes."

"Yes, it is, my answer is yes, definitely yes!" He had paperwork for me to sign and fill out. He gave me information about packing my photographs and frames and how to insure them with my insurance company. It was great information to know before I made calls on such short notice.

"Right now, our plans are to fly out Wednesday sometime, that way I'd be there Thursday before noon to set up my exhibit. I would love for you to join us for this exciting opportunity if you can free your schedule at such short notice. I respect your experience and professionalism and input would be invaluable."

"I will bring my girlfriend and we will be there to help Thursday. Let me give you my cell number so we can be in contact in New York." He gave me his number, and I gave him mine and Jacobs in case I didn't have my phone, Jacob always has his. I was so excited I could hardly sit still.

I picked up my phone and without thinking, I called

Brandon. My first photography instructor and got his voicemail. I said "Brandon, this is Jenna, and I have great news. I have a photography exhibit in New York City at the Art Institute this weekend. I just wanted to thank you for helping me get to this point. You are a great instructor and I benefited greatly. Thanks again."

I hung up the phone and realized what I had just done. I called without asking Jacob first, oh no, no, no what can of worms did I just open! What was I thinking? Oh I know, I wasn't thinking. Jacob he will, I honestly don't know what he will do. I do know I'm in serious trouble!

I got home and Jacob had flowers for me when I walked in the door. He is going to kill me for sharing this special moment with another man. I had to tell him what I did.

"Thank you for the beautiful bouquet of flowers. And thank you for sharing in my excitement and making it special by going with me. But I've done something I need to tell you so you might want to sit down. I wasn't thinking".

Jacob sat down on the couch and looked penetrating at me, "what is it?"

"Jacob, sweetheart, after I talked to you on the phone, and I had told my professor our decision to participate in the exhibit, I was so excited in the car and I..."

"Jenna, stop pacing back and forth and just tell me, what happened, what did you do?"

"I was so excited, I wasn't thinking, and I called Brandon to tell him my good news. He was my first photography instructor and I thought I owed him a thank you for helping me get started in this field.

I didn't talk to him personally, I just left a message on his voicemail, but I didn't even think about getting permission from you until after I had hung up and realized what I'd done. I don't want to get back with him. It was just that I was so thankful for this opportunity, and I wanted to thank him. That's all it was." I looked at him, waiting for something to hit the fan.

"Jenna, that's so you. You have this amazing opportunity to be recognized for your work, and you are thinking of others who have helped you get to where you are? How could you think I'd be mad at you for being the person I love? He is your past and I know that and trust you. Thank you for telling me and I'm sorry you were worried to tell me what you did. You can tell me anything, anytime. I am here for you."

"I know that Jacob, and I love you so much. Have you been to New York before?"

"No, you?"

"Nope. I'm so excited we are New York virgins together. This should be fun. What reservations do we need to arrange?" Jacob offered to fly us to New York but said it would be much cheaper for us both to fly first class than take his plane, so I was thrilled.

He had Twyla his secretary book our flights. He said he could always cancel them if I wanted something else. I ran upstairs to look in my closet for what to wear. I tried on my white dress I wore for our wedding. I tried it on, but it was too big on me, I came out and asked Jacob if it looked good and he looked concerned.

"You have got to start eating. You are skin and bones you are losing all the curves that dress is just hanging on you. You have to stay healthy for me, you have to eat."

Well great, I have the dress I wore when I went dancing with Andrew and Eddie, but that night was so negative should I even try it on? Yes, let's see that dress. I put it on and it was looser than when I wore it last. Jacob noticed too but didn't say so.

"Jenna, that is truly a sexy dress, but you need a different dress, one that makes you feel special. We can go to town tomorrow and get you a new outfit for your New York debut. But first we are going to eat dinner, something fattening."

"Sure, I'm hungry, what do you want me to fix? We have left over ham we could have mac and cheese and ham. Sound good to you?"

"Yes babe, sounds like a fattening mix of carbs and protein. I'll set the table."

"Thanks, we are such a good team."

After we ate, we called and reserved our hotel, rental car and Jacob got tickets to see the musical Wicked the prequel of the Wizard of Oz, and Hamilton. Both Broadway shows should be great to see. I'm just glad my country boy is willing to do these things with me. He is my best friend and takes great care of me. This is so exciting and so unexpected!

Jacob and I went to bed excited for the activities and experiences facing us in the next few days. We went to bed and celebrated in our private ways our excitement for my shocking photography opportunity.

The next day Jacob and I had a big breakfast then into town to shop for a dress. We went to a wedding store just in case they might have some extra special dresses for my special occasion. They had two that I really liked. One was a deep bright blue leather dress, the length was about one hand above the knees, and it was the softest leather I'd ever felt.

It was very expensive, but Jacob loved it. It did fit like a glove, but I think leather is supposed to fit like a glove. The other dress was a deep magenta color with a thin black pin stripe, and it was a much shorter dress about six to eight inches above my knees.

This dress looked like the arts, unique and expensive. I thought my black patent two-inch heels would look great with both dresses. Jacob thought I should buy both of them one to wear on Friday night and one for Saturday. I agreed and we walked out with two great dresses.

"Jacob, do you need to buy a tux or suit for the fancy New York weekend"?

"No, I haven't lost weight and my clothes aren't falling off me, so I don't need to buy new clothes. I'll bring a suit".

While in town, I had a fake spray tan done. I also worked in an appointment to have my fingers and toenails painted. I was ready for our trip, so as the song says, "start spreading the news, I'm going to be a part of it, New York, New York."

Jacob was on his laptop while he was waiting for me, getting all this stuff done. I was glad he was able to use this time getting prepped for his work and still be with me. Big Apple here we come!

CHAPTER 6

The Exhibit

I talked with my professor, and he divulged the contact names and numbers for the gallery, Dane Bradley, and Melissa Hawdeck. He gave me their numbers if I ran into any problems. Jacob brought his laptop and did work on the flight, but he was helpful to make sure my art was insured, packed and flown with the utmost care.

I relaxed on the flight even had a couple of glasses of wine (I don't know why I ordered wine, it gives me a headache every time, but it just seemed like the grown up professional drink I should drink). I love flying in first class, and next to my handsome husband who is my security blanket. I can't believe my art is going to be seen in New York City.

I'd called my mom and Jeff and got their congratulations. Jeff and his wife were going to try to fly out to see my exhibit, but Jeff hates New York, how is that possible? I'm not sure he will make it out here for the showing because of the late notice. I don't expect anyone to come really, it's just the honor of being asked.

I know I'm blessed to be married to a man who can afford to splurge and do fun exciting things like this. I didn't tell my uncles and my aunt because they had so many expenses lately with Grandpas' funeral and Grandma's legal expenses and her funeral, that I didn't want them to know because they would make personal sacrifices to come out and support me.

I thought I'd just take pictures and tell them all about it after the fact. Jacob was on Skype with Fred his business partner and another businessman and when they were saying goodbye and the other man was off the connection, Fred asked Jacob if he would turn the screen so he could see what I was wearing, if I was wearing anything at all. I heard him and commented, "very funny Fred". He laughed and I still can't see Fred or talk to him without a blush first.

I quickly poked my head into the computer camera and said, "by the way, just so you know, Jacob loved that red hot lover naughty nighty." He blushed, and I was the last one laughing on that deal! It's a good thing I can laugh at my stupid mistakes.

The plane landed and we went straight to the customer service desk to find out where my artwork would be unloaded. The Art Gallery had a truck scheduled to meet us at the airport to pick-up and deliver my art pieces to the Gallery. We showed our official paperwork and were allowed to go down to the loading zone and verify that all my pieces were accounted for and loaded in the truck for drop off and delivery.

That took a load off my mind to know they had arrived safe, and sound and that the Gallery had them. All I had to do now was to hang them and adjust the lighting for them tomorrow. So exciting, I'm with the most wonderful man in the world, in one of the most exciting cities in the country, I am living large.

Speaking of large, I'm starving. I always wanted to eat

in the Tavern on the Greens at Central Park but that place closed many years ago so we picked a spot in the must see from Former's New York Guide to the city.

We dropped our stuff off in our room at the hotel, and seriously after Bora Bora no room will ever measure up to the first class views and comforts. But our room was nice and upscale just generic. There were snacks in our welcome basket in the room, so we munched and crunched with waters and it hit the spot.

We unpacked our luggage, plugged in our devices and I threw down the bedspread to make sure the sheets were clean. Then we had intimate time together before our New York city adventure. After our expression of love, we jumped into the shower. Once refreshed we were ready to explore New York.

"Jacob this can't be a second honeymoon, because I won't have the strength to walk all over this town. We need food, no more snacks, I need real food." He just laughed. We threw on our jeans I dried my hair, threw on my make-up and put on comfortable walking shoes. I wanted to walk around and tour the Big Apple.

We ate at a New York Style pizza by the slice vendor on the street, and it was delicious. The one slice of pizza was like the size of half a pizza back home, and it was seriously so good I ate one and a half slices. Jacob finished the rest of my second piece. It was so flavorful, I love pizza, but this was primo! My stomach literally hurt but I could not stop. We shared a Cannoli for dessert, I loved it, he didn't like it, so I ate more than my half.

So far in the food department, New York is a four-star eatery for me. It could be I was just really hungry, but I enjoyed the experience. We walked downtown and there were open air market spaces with people selling fake Prada, Coach, Rolex you name it they were trying to sell it.

I did find some rings I liked. They were silver with turquoise, mother of pearl, pearl, and a red jade ring that was unique. My fingers were smaller than they used to be, and I could use some rings now. I had a great time shopping and Jacob was a great sport to be my walking and shopping buddy. He was just glad I bought small items, so it wasn't heavy to carry all over the city.

I wanted to walk over the Brooklyn Bridge. I'd seen it in several movies and wanted that experience with the man I loved. Jacob was in his boots but they are like tennis shoes to him, they are his comfortable shoes, so we walked hand in hand over the bridge and then back. I must admit it was much further than it looked when we first started walking.

Jacob slowed down our pace coming back because he could see I was out of shape. He jogs almost every morning with his Dalmatian Charlie, and that must be how he keeps so fit and in good shape. I need to start exercising so I can keep up with him.

We had a full day and I was ready to go back to our room and snuggle with my honey and get a good night sleep before my big day tomorrow. When back in our room, I took off my jeans and my legs were exhausted. Between two rounds of sex and walking all over the city for hours, my legs were killing me.

We both grabbed waters and plopped our bodies into the hot pulsating bubbles of the hot tub in the corner of our room. When I got out, my legs were still rubbery like I had no bones left in my legs. I was so tired we decided to just go to bed early. We set our phones for wake-up alarms before sleeping.

Jacob turned on the T.V and I fell asleep. He had a T.V in his bedroom before I moved in, but I persuaded him to remove the television from our bedroom and that was a change he wasn't thrilled about at first. But he had adjusted and our bedroom time is our intimate, private time and I don't have to share him with every super model that is coming on T.V. selling something. I'm not as dumb as I look, T.V. out of the bedroom.

With the excitement of New York and my exciting day tomorrow it was hard to turn my thoughts off and get to sleep, but I'm the type of person who needs sleep to stay healthy. Ever since my cancer surgeries, I don't have the energy I used to without plenty of sleep. I'm an eight hour a night girl.

Anyway, I was sound asleep and so was my husband and sometime in the early morning I woke up with excruciating painful leg cramps. I jumped out of bed, disoriented with the new room surroundings, trying to find a light and get my leg from cramping. This had never happened to me before, and Jacob was up with the light on and he was looking all around the room trying to figure out what was going on. Jacob I'm so sorry I woke you. It's my leg, it's cramping so bad, and I can't get it to uncramp.

Jacob immediately got on the hotel phone and asked for room service to send a banana, cereal and a glass of milk and if it's here in 5 minutes or less, there will be a $20 tip. He slipped on his jeans and told me to stay out of eye sight or put on a robe. I saw that there were hotel robes, so I put one on, and it was soft and I like warm so it was a good choice. The food was at our door in less than two minutes. Jacob just smiled and said, "money talks in New York City too, babe."

"Yes, the universal language."

"You need to eat the banana to get rid of your leg cramps, but the cereal is to get down the banana." How could he think so clearly so quickly in the middle of the night or whenever it was? I love this man. He was rubbing my legs and I was finally getting relief. I ate the early breakfast and felt much better. I ate the entire banana but couldn't eat all the cereal. Jacob finished the cereal off for me. It was 3:49 a.m. when I finished my breakfast.

"Sweetheart, do you think you could go back to sleep now if I turned off the lights?"

"Yes, I think we should both try to sleep, we have a long

day ahead of us tomorrow or should I say today." I got into bed, Jacob turned off the lights and we curled up together and slept until our alarms went off.

He had set the alarm on his phone, and it was going off on the nightstand on the left of the bed, and the phone was ringing on the right nightstand, it was like stereo wake up sounds, sort of alarming. Jacob had turned off his phone, and I leaned over to kiss him, and he felt hot. I sat straight up in bed, "Jacob, are you feeling, okay?"

"I'm really thirsty." I jumped up and ran to the fridge grabbed a bottled water and came over to him. My heart was in my throat, I need him, he can't be sick. I don't want him sick, he's never sick. "What can I do for you?"

"Do you have any Tylenol?"

"Yes," I ran to my purse and gave him two extra strength pills.

"I'm going to sleep while you take your shower."

"Do you need to eat something to take those pills Honey? I don't want you to be sick. I'll call room service and get you some food."

"No, you get something for you to eat, I'll just rest here a little bit longer and I'll be fine."

I called room service and ordered thinking it's a big hotel and it will take them a while to fix it and deliver it. I told them we needed eggs, crisp bacon, sausage patties, two orange juices, two coffees with creamers, croissants with fresh fruit. I just got my clothes off and was stepping into the shower when there was a knock on the door.

I quickly threw my robe back on and it was room service. I guess the crew talked about the $20 tip for quick service earlier, so these kids were literally flying to get us what we wanted when we wanted it. So much for my plan, I walked over to get a tip and the smallest cash I had was a ten spot, so I just gave it to him and he smiled, thanked me and closed the door behind him. Each dish had a warmer cover on top.

I asked Jacob if he wanted to eat now or wait until my shower? But he was already sleeping, so I went back to the shower to refresh and pray for my husband. I know Jacob and even if he's sicker than a dog, he will say he feels fine, so he can be my helper for today. While I was in the bathroom, I decided a plan.

I am a block and a half walk to the Art Gallery, thanks to my husband's good planning. I can let him sleep, walk over there and get my art hung and ready for the show. Then I'll come back to the room and take care of my sick husband. I was dressed and ready to go and came out of the bathroom and Jacob was sitting up in bed eating his breakfast.

"Nice try handsome, but you are not leaving this room today."

"I'm fine, I just needed some extra sleep, my temperature is normal, and I feel fine."

"You would look me in the eyes and lie to be there for me today, I know you. But baby I want to take care of you. You've never been sick before since I've been with you, and I want to take care of you."

"Correction, I have been sick in the hospital, and you were there 24/7 with me, didn't eat or change your clothes for three days. I know you put me first babe, but really, I'm fine. You take good care of me."

"If you are up to it, how about we walk down the block to the exhibit, come in with me to see what's happening and where, then come back to the room and rest. I will call you when I'm ready to walk back to the hotel and you can walk and meet me, and we can do lunch together and see how you are feeling from there."

"You don't need to spend your time and energy worrying about me, I really am fine."

"I know you are fine, every time I look at you, I see fine in a million ways."

"That's as hot as biting your bottom lip so you better eat

your breakfast if you don't want your clothes off in a pile in the immediate future."

I do want that, but you need your strength, so I just laughed and started eating. He did look better; he had color back in his cheeks, and his eyes looked whiter too not so yellowish, he looks like he's feeling better. Maybe he is better.

Jacob ate quickly and jumped into the shower. He was washed dried and dressed in less than 30 minutes. He's so good looking, I just wanted to stay. I couldn't take it, I walked over and put one hand in his hair, then my other hand, and put both my elbows on the top of his shoulders and pulled myself up on him. I wrapped my legs around him and I kissed him. I kissed his eyes, his nose, his lips, and then he says, "Jenna, I told you I don't have a temperature."

"You may not, but you've given me one." He just chuckled and carried me to the bed. We had a mid-morning ron-day-vew. What a great way to start our day. I went back to the bathroom to freshen up, and after we were clean and re-dressed, we headed out for the Art Gallery.

"I don't expect you to stay here all day with me, I don't know what I'll be doing or how long it will take, so if you want to bring your laptop to do your work, I am totally fine with you doing that. Or you could come back to the room and work here. Whatever you want babe, that's what I want."

"I know, and since you are okay with it, I will take my laptop and if I'm not needed, then I will sit in a corner somewhere and work while I watch you do your thing."

"Sounds like a plan. Thanks for sharing this exciting moment for me. It wouldn't mean anything without you here to share it with me. I love you so much."

"I love you too."

"Can I ask you a serious question before we leave our beautiful hotel room?"

"Of course, what do you want to know?"

"Well sometimes if you say something over and over it doesn't mean as much, but I find myself telling you that I love you all the time because I can't find any other words to express how much you mean to me. My question is "would it mean more to you if I didn't say it so often or is it still meaningful when I share those words from my heart to you?"

Jacob scooted off the bed took me in his arms and held me close as he whispered in my ear, "Jenna, I love hearing that you love me. It means more to me than I know how to express. Every time you say those words it makes me happy to my very core.

So, to answer your serious question, no you don't say it too often and yes, it means the world to me when you say those words because I know you mean them. It reminds me how lucky we are to have each other." Now we need to go so you can be on time for your art show meeting.

"Okay and thank you for loving me, I still don't get how I got so lucky, but I adore who you are and who we are when we are together."

"You need to stop being affectionate because we have to leave this room right now or you will miss your art opportunity."

Jacob let go of our embrace, we didn't even kiss because we both knew we would end up back in bed, so we just walked to the elevator.

While we were walking our block and a half to the Gallery, I called my professor and told him I was almost to the gallery. He asked what took me so long, that he was sitting outside on the steps waiting for me. He brought me a coffee and was looking handsome and excited on the front steps. He didn't have his girlfriend with him, she was sleeping at their hotel, so I introduced Jacob to my instructor.

"Sorry, I didn't know if you drank coffee."

Jacob said, "no problem, thanks for getting Jenna one, she loves her coffee." I felt uncomfortable for a moment, then I thanked him for my coffee, put my arm in my husbands' arm and said, ready or not, here we come. And we started walking up the stairs to the Art exhibitor entrance.

I squealed out loud with excitement and Jacob squeezed my hand. I didn't mean to do it, it just sort of jumped out of me, this was not even a dream I would have wished for myself, and here it is, another unbelievable moment, this is real and happening and I have Jacob to share my special moment.

We were greeted at the front doors with security and Dane was our guide for the day. Melissa was working with another artist for the gallery event, so Dane would be our go to man for anything we needed. He showed us my little area at the gallery that I would have to display my prints and there was wire, nails, lights, and all my art leaning against the wall, etc.

I asked for paint. Dane asked what color I wanted for the background wall color. I said pale yellow cream, just not a white wall to hang my art on. I want them to see my art not the wall behind them, but white walls, my art would never hang on a white wall. Spoken like a true artist.

Dane said, "You have a couple of nice pieces." I didn't know if it was a compliment or a slam, so I just smiled and said "thanks." I was really glad Jacob was here because he helped us hang wires to adjust the lights to shine just where I wanted them to be on each picture. I thought it would be half a day for Dane to get my paint, but he was back in about ten minutes with the paint.

I quickly painted my backdrop and arranged my pieces on the floor, so I'd know where I wanted them arranged on the walls after the paint dried. My gallery location was toward the very back corner of the institute, but I didn't care, I'm here and it's an extreme honor.

Dane asked, "Are your pieces for sale? People normally ask and I needed a price for each piece so I can be prepared for the public."

I looked at Jacob, I had not planned on selling my work, but I guess that's what is expected. I asked if I had time to walk around and see how other works of art are priced.

"Sure, take thirty minutes and walk around, just don't touch anything." While my paint was drying, my husband and I were walking around the gallery hand in hand exploring artistic expressions from people all over the world.

It was amazing to see up close magnificent art. My instructor found us in the maze of art exhibits and asked what price range I was considering. I told him and he grinned and said, well you can always come down. I just looked at Jacob, and he squeezed my hand.

"Jenna, it's your art, your vision and if someone wants it, they will pay your price. If you want to keep all your pieces, you have the space at home to hang and display your work, I could display your work at my offices, so there is no pressure for you to sell or give away anything you don't want to."

"Thanks, I'm so glad you are here with me." My instructor Darren wanted me to know that the paint was dry, and now that it was dry, he thought that the color was a good choice.

"Thanks, I'm glad you approve." So we moved up to my pieces and Jacob had a level and they were marking nails and hanging and reinforcing wires to ensure the work if bumped or touched that it would be sturdy and secure. We got the last things hung and it was 5:50.

Jacob had worked so hard today. I don't know what I would have done without him. I can't draw a straight line with a ruler, so thank God he was here to make sure my final presentation looked professional. I was exhausted but pleased with the final look. I took some pictures with my phone.

Dane sternly commented, "You can't use a flash in here."

"Sorry, it won't happen again." I've found it's easier to ask forgiveness than to get permission sometimes. We gave Dane back all the building supplies we didn't need anymore, and he said that my space would be cleaned up and that there would be a red carpet on the floor in front of my work. I asked if it could be a deep green even a grassy looking carpet instead of a red carpet, and he said that could be arranged.

Because of my pickiness, another delay for dinner. I went back with Dane to pick out the floor runner color. I found the perfect green grassy feel I wanted in front of my nature photographs. My back to nature theme feels much better with a green grassy path to follow rather than looking at a floor of red carpet.

Now I'm ready to relax and celebrate. Darren got at least one buzzing text an hour from his girlfriend, Kim. I didn't know if his girlfriend was board, or if he's just that busy. I thanked him for his help and for him recommending my work for this display. He just looked at me and Jacob grinned and walked away. Sort of an odd response, but I just thought he was tired and, in a hurry, to get to Kim.

We were told to bring photo identification and to use the east entrance when we came back for the featured exhibits tomorrow evening. We were ready for the show, and I was ready to go. We walked outside the institute and I just jumped up into Jacob's arms and started kissing him. My instructor just walked off and muttered, "enthusiastic minx?" When I finished kissing Jacob, he said "let's get some food, you haven't had lunch and now it's past dinner."

"That sounds good to me." We went back to the hotel, I felt bad that Jacob didn't get any of his work done today on his computer, but thank God he was my handy man. I was so glad he was feeling better too. I felt his head and he wasn't hot, I figured if the fever reducer would have worn off by now, but his forehead was cool to the kiss.

I rewarded him for his hard work in the shower, and he seemed well compensated for his efforts. When he groans in his low soft release of passion, there are waves of satisfaction and desire that roll in whip like speed inside of me and floods through my entire body, but always starting and ending at my heart. I love him so completely.

We made it out of the large shower and got dressed. I take longer to get ready because my hair is longer, I keep threatening to get it cut, but Jacob always says please don't, I love your hair. I can't do it, not because I don't have the control, but because I want to please him more than I want to make my life easier.

I heard him on the phone confirming reservations as I was coming out of the bathroom. He smells so good, and looks so handsome, how did I ever, ever, ever get so lucky to be with a man as good looking as him? I am really living a dream life, and I never want to wake up.

Del Posto, was a great dining experience. The food four star and so romantic with my handsome husband. He wore a black pair of jeans, boots of course, white button down shirt and a black leather blazer and with his blue eyes and dark wavy hair, he looked like a magazine cover. I spend much time and energy on my hair, make-up and even with all the primping, I pale in the shadow of his gorgeousness.

I had a short black skirt with large flat pleats, a white and black horizontal wide striped cotton long sleeved blouse and little electric blue blazer that came to my waist, it was one of a kind. I wore my new onyx ear rings and my new red jade ring on one hand and my wedding ring on the other. I looked up at Jacob and he was just smiling at me. "What are you thinking?"

"I'm thinking that I know why you like to run around naked all the time."

"I don't run around naked all the time, but I'm curious as to why you think that?"

"Because you look better naked than any other way I know. Clothes just cover your natural beauty, you are hot!"

"Baby, you need an eye exam, and I don't run around naked all the time. Don't you like my outfit? You should have told me I would have worn something else."

"You know I like anything you wear. You always look beautiful."

"Jacob, honestly are you okay? I really want you to feel good. Do you want to go back to the room and rest, or go to a club? What do you want to do? This entire day has been all about me, I want to do something for you."

"I think you already did that in the shower, and I must say you showed skills that will be used again and soon. But seriously I don't want you to overdo it. I don't want you to wake up in three hours crying and jumping around the room, you scared me last night with your leg cramp."

"Sorry about that, I'd never had a leg cramp wake me up in my sleep before, and it was just as shocking for me too."

Chapter 7

New York City

"We could stop at an off-Broadway club and listen to some live music for a while and have a couple of drinks. While in Rome?"

"Sure, that would be fun. Any particular club you have in mind?"

"Let's ask a waiter or waitress here to see if they have any recommendations." We asked three different servers and they all said the same place. We put the name in our and smartphone GPS locators and we were off to the subway then walking to a fun club. It was a piano bar and had an off-Broadway solo woman singer.

As we walked in the door, the space was small and cozy. We walked down into what was probably a studio apartment at one time, maybe back in the 1950's and they had decorated the place with red walls, black leather chairs, and a black laminate bar along most of the left side of the club.

It had tables squeezed together to get the most amount

of people together, and a black grand piano at the back right section of the club on a slightly elevated stage. The entire back wall was mirrors so it wasn't a dark hole like a typical bar. It was more like an old movie saloon, retro and tacky but somehow for this area it worked.

The woman who was the star came out in a long sequenced black gown that came to the floor. It was a low cut "V-neck" and she had curves to fill out the dress in an upscale sexy style. She wore red lipstick to match the red walls and decorations of the club. Her lips were so red it was extreme fake and distracting from her beautiful voice.

She had volume, and a range from high soprano to low alto, maybe even a low baritone. But I couldn't get past her lips they were so distracting. She had the reddest lipstick color I'd ever seen. Her hair was died so black and her face was so porcelain white that she looked like a comic figure. She was a visual distraction to such an amazing voice. It was like a clown singing opera, but I couldn't look away.

Such extreme hair color, jet black not natural looking at all, her make-up was white as paper white to make her color white and not flesh colored and the lips, she clearly wanted to make an impression to be memorable. And that she was, but I felt sorry for her.

It took extreme effort on my part to get past her looks to enjoy her beautiful voice. She had striking features, a pretty woman, but she had bad advisors in the make-up department. She had a beautiful tone, vibrato, good pitch, voice control and range she was very talented musically.

The baby grand piano was up on a black wooden platform about a foot higher than the rest of the club. The place being small became like one big family atmosphere as the drinks poured everyone joined in on certain songs. We were practically related by the time we left at closing time. We had stayed much longer than we had expected, and we were glad to have been part of the New York culture, if only for a short time.

I was ready for bed by the time we finally reached our hotel. Jacob and I had walked back to our hotel and pretty much dropped our clothes off on the floor and crashed in bed. I woke up to kissing, and I opened my eyes, and it was clear that Jacob was not only awake, but he was really feeling better today, much more energy and I was happy with my wake-up booty call. I love being married I really do love this man, what he does to me! Today is going to be a great day. No today is already a great day.

We were free to walk around and enjoy the city all day as long as we were at the institute by 6:00 p.m. Things don't happen early in New York City. New York is a night owl type of city and I loved it. The people we've been in contact with were all friendly and I've felt safe on the subways, walking, everywhere we've gone.

We decided to ride the Stanton Island Ferry and go see the Statue of Liberty. I can't believe we are here and I didn't bring my camera. Just my phone camera, what a dork! There were extremely long lines to get up close to the statue, so we just rode the ferry back and shopped and walked and ate at a New York style hot dog shop.

This is what I call a hot dog, the best I've ever tasted. I would never lose weight in this city. I would be in better shape because people here walk everywhere. I really like this city, from a tourist's perspective this is a great place I would recommend visiting this city in a "New York minute."

We went to a wax museum and took phone pictures of us with the stars, we were going to go to the Jimmy Fallon's taping of his show but changed our minds when we saw the lines and people. We were going to have people around us all night at the exhibit. We decided to go back to our room, eat some New York Cheesecake in bed, maybe take a nap then get ready for my first and probably only professional art exhibit.

I was so excited. Okay it was me who wanted the

cheesecake, but the strawberries and diet dr. pepper was a win, win addition. I took a nap and Jacob was on his computer when I went to sleep. When I woke up, he was in the same spot. I felt bad that I was putting him behind at work.

"Hi sweetheart, are you very far behind in your work because of me?"

"I'm not behind anything except behind my wife, supporting her. My work is fine, I have good people working for me and they can manage the slack, enjoy your day. Are you ready for a great night tonight?"

"We need to eat something for protein because that sweet cheesecake made me hungry." It was four o'clock and we had an hour to get a block down the street to the exhibit. I'm not sure why we have to be there so early, but I'll go with the flow. We ordered cheese burgers and fries. I wanted onion rings but didn't want to have onion breath for the evening, so I went with fries. They were good.

Jacob wanted me to drink a couple bottles of water before we left for the evening so I wouldn't get dehydrated. I was afraid it would make me have to go to the bathroom all night long, but I drank the water for him. I trusted him and wanted to please him.

My professor Darren Ray, called and said his girlfriend Kim was running late, so he wouldn't be at the entrance at 5:30. I told him I'd pass on his information to the door keepers. He said thanks and hung up.

"Jacob, he sounded stressed on the phone. I don't feel stressed at all. I know we've done all the work, now it's just stand back, and enjoy the experience, right?"

"Right babe, you enjoy every second of your night. Come here." He turned the computer off and while we were waiting for our dinner, we had a private celebration, I love it when Jacob is away from his work, he's so much more relaxed and attentive to us. All the sex could be another reason, but he really is more relaxed, and I love it!"

The knock at the door let us know our food was ready. I pulled up the covers, Jacob threw on his jeans and answered the door in his sexed up hair, and I just lay in the bed and giggled like a school girl. He is so handsome; I've never seen him look anyway but gorgeous.

We ate dinner in bed then I jumped in the shower and started the high power work to be picture perfect for my photo exhibit. I decided on my blue leather dress and Jacob had talked to Dane about what to wear and he said that a tux would be over dressed, but a suit, or jeans and an upscale jacket would be in line with what would be expected. He said people dress up for these exhibits.

Jacob asked me if he should wear his jeans or suit. I love him in a suit, but he'd be much more comfortable in his boots and jeans, so I suggested he wear his black jeans, black blazer and blue dress shirt coordinated with my dress and he looked like a knockout as always. He takes my breath away. I was standing looking at him in the mirror and holding my heart. He saw me looking at him, and just shook his head, "Jenna, get ready."

He was right, I just needed a few more attempts at my make-up and lip gloss and I'd be ready. I sprayed my hair spray and perfume, now I'm ready to go. I slipped on my pumps and we were ready to leave, and had fifteen minutes to spare for a five minute walk. We were good to go. Tummy's full, looking good, and feeling fine. Tonight, is mine, and the love of my life is with me, to share this once in a lifetime experience.

CHAPTER 8

An Unexpected Turn of Events

We got to the event and other people were there who had displays in the building as well. There were lots of smiles and excitement and there were clearly snobby individuals and only name brand people. A dressy woman, very classy looking, walked up to Jacob and asked him if he was a model? Then she asked him if he'd like to be?

I quickly pushed in between where she was standing and Jacob and got in her face and said, "he's married to me, so try that line on a single man and walk away please." Jacob just laughed out loud and as the woman was quietly walking away. Jacob put his hand on my shoulder and turned me around to face him.

"Jenna, you crack me up. I don't think she was coming on to me, I think she may have been serious."

"Well sorry to spoil your modeling career, but I don't care who she is, she was in your personal space, and your personal space is mine too. I couldn't stand by and watch her violate you like that."

"Jenna" (Jacob was shaking his head no and trying to hold back cracking up out loud) "thanks for protecting me babe."

"Let's move and go stand over there where people look more down to earth, not so uppity. I clearly am comfortable just being me, clean, dressed up and not taking this entire art exhibit too seriously." Just enjoying the journey with Jacob at my side, arm around my neck, and I loved him being here with me. I whispered in his ear, which I could do much easier than usual in my two-inch pumps, "thank you for loving me and sharing this moment with me. With you here, by my side, this moment is perfect. But I do have one request."

He stood back and looked serious, "sure name it."

"When people get here tonight, don't stand by my art. They will see how handsome you are, and no one will look at my pictures, they will just be staring at you, you are so beautiful."

Jacob just smiled and grabbed me and pulled me to him and was kissing me passionately. I regained my composure and pulled myself away from him. There was an announcement asking us to stand by our exhibits and that the doors would open in five minutes.

I wanted to make one last bathroom break before the person or persons arrived. I stood in my high heels and not many people were here when it opened. I was wishing I had a chair or comfortable shoes on, but I could manage a few hours in heels. I saw my instructor and his girlfriend she looked really young, good luck with that arm candy Dr. Ray.

I told Jacob he was free to walk around and see the displays now that everyone has their final projects up. He said he was right where he wanted to be and in ear shot if I needed him for anything. I had to smile because I knew he meant it.

Jacob leaned over to my professor and boldly proclaimed, "I take it that Jenna is getting an "A" in your class with all this extra credit and notoriety for you and your school."

The professor just looked at Jacob and said, "yes." I just laughed at my husband taking control of the situation.

I heard the sound of laughing men's voices, all low tones, and sounds of cowboy boots walking on carpet around the corner and here they were the whole Jamison clan, all the brothers and Jacob's dad walked in with girlfriends on their arms too. They were all smiles like they'd just won the lottery.

I was very surprised to see them, it was so sweet of them all to come and support me. I can't believe they left the farm to come to New York City. I didn't even tell them. Jacob must have told them. I gave his dad a big hug and kiss and he just smiled.

He looked at my prints and said, "you've represented the family and Kentucky well." That was the most his dad had said to me ever, and it was so thoughtful and kind.

"Thanks dad!" He just stared at me. I said, "Oh I'm sorry should I not call you dad?"

"No, it's not that, it's just I've never had a woman call me dad before, remember no girls."

"Well then I will have a special place in your heart and that suits me just fine." And I hugged him again. I looked at Jacob and both his eyes were full of water. I thought I would cry if my husband cried, but I just winked at Jacob over his dad's shoulder.

I looked at his brother's and they were all staring at me and all silent, with these guys that does not happen often. I guess they didn't have a lot of experience seeing their dad affectionate and tender toward someone. I felt I needed to say something.

I said "Thank you all for coming tonight, I really am surprised and thrilled that you would go out of your way to make me feel special. Thank you and feel free to ask questions and see the other artist's pieces. There are some really creative, talented and amazing works in here."

I hadn't spoken to Andrew since he'd asked me to forgive him as part of his A.A. twelve steps. I don't know how many steps he needed to make or if there are different numbers of steps for different people's needs, but the program really seemed to be helping him. He was a kind and caring guy and even his skin coloring was a healthier color now, I was sincerely happy for him.

Eddie gave me a big hug and I hugged and kissed him on the lips. I felt closest to him, he'd seen me at my worst and helped me stay sane, so I was thrilled to see him. He just blushed and looked at Jacob.

Jacob just stared at him and raised an eyebrow, and Eddie raised both of his hands in the air like he was under arrest. I just laughed out loud and then the rest did too. It was like a Jamison family reunion in the back corner of the gallery and if they are the only ones who see my work, I am fine with that.

Then I heard a familiar voice "Hey Sis!" I looked and there was Jeff, and my mom. Oh my word, I rushed over and gave hugs and kisses and showed them my work. They were both so sweet to come and support my special debut.

I asked Jacob if he could find a chair for my mom because she had to do a lot of walking to get to the back of the gallery. She was all dressed up and in dress shoes, so I knew her feet would be hurting her. I wanted my mom to be comfortable so she could enjoy the night.

He punched Andrew and the two of them walked off to locate Dane. I was telling them about my pictures and mom needed to use the restroom. I told her I needed to stay with my exhibit, but two of Jacob's brother's girlfriends said they'd go with her if I wanted them too. It was nice, sort of breaking up the crowd of family. It must have built excitement with all the family back with me because more people were coming back to see my work now that it was getting later in the evening.

Then I heard her sweet young voice call out my name, Miss. Jenna? I looked up and it was Kourtney and Brandon. They came all the way to New York City to be there for me. Kourtney ran up to me and I hugged and I kissed her. She had grown a foot since I had seen her last.

And Brandon looked thinner than I remembered but still as handsome as ever. I hugged and kissed him and thanked him for coming. My kiss was a brotherly, so glad you're here kiss. But he pulled me back to him and kissed me like I miss my lover kiss.

Here I was surrounded by Jacobs' family and mine, and his daughter and here he was kissing me with passion, Jacob will kill him. I was pushing him away but it wasn't working. All of a sudden, Jacob was between me and Brandon. "Jacob please, I called and invited him to see my exhibit. Have you met his daughter; this is Miss. Kourtney"? I took Jacob's hand and lead him away from Brandon.

Brandon said, "I'm sorry Jenna, I didn't mean to do that." Jacob just turned around and glared him down. I just replied, "Boys play nice," and continued walking Jacob away from Brandon.

Jacob stopped turned back around and said, "Nice to meet you Miss. Kourtney I've heard only good things about you." Kourtney was all smiles and said, "Thank you." She was caught up in my hot husband's looks. Any woman would be, and a high school girl wouldn't have a chance against his rugged good looks and piercing white beautiful smile.

Jacob whispered in my ear, "Jenna this is your night and I'm here to support you. Your family loves you and they are here too. But if you ever kiss Brandon again, in my presence or not, I will do prison time for my actions, do you hear and understand me?"

I didn't argue, I just said "Yes dear."

Then he whispered "Jenna, refocus don't let one jerk steal away the fun of your night. Just erase those last five minutes and do your thing and shine." I didn't know if I liked the prison time reference, but I'll deal with all this conversation later.

Brandon liked my work, he asked great questions, and I introduced him to my current professor Dr. Ray, and they visited together for quite a while. Kourtney was staring at all of Jacob's handsome single brothers, so I motioned for Andrew to see if he would walk around with Kourtney to show her the exhibits. She jumped at the opportunity to be on the arm of one of Jacob's handsome brothers. Brandon just stared at me and nodded an okay.

Jacob gave me my space but was never out of peripheral vision. About three hours into the viewing, a distinguished woman came up to me and offered to buy all my prints. She has an interior design company and wanted my works for her clients. She wanted to know if I could work a better price if she bought them all. I said I'd have to ask my financial advisor and I motioned for Jacob to come over. He was attentive and walked over with style and power.

I introduced first names only and told him her proposition. He said we've had offers and interest all night long and if you want original work by Jenna, the price is as marked. Then Jacob turned and walked over to my professor and Brandon and looked like they were talking business. So the lady said your business partner is smart and handsome. I want the prints so just tell me who to make the check-out to, and consider these prints sold.

"I will introduce you to Dane Bradley, and he will assist you with the sale and prints. Thank you so much for loving my work. Feel free to contact me if you are looking for other prints in the future."

She shook my hand and said that she would be in touch. We had an agreement that the photos would stay on display until after Saturday's exhibit's close and the institute would repack the prints and send them to the buyers address(s). The woman walked off around the corner, and I just ran over to Jacob and said, "you were amazing Jacob, she bought them all."

Then I noticed something in the way Jacob smiled at me, I had a sick thought, "gentlemen would you excuse Jacob and me for a moment?"

"Sure."

I pulled him around the corner and asked him one question. "Jacob, tell me you didn't have anything to do with that woman offering to buy my work."

I could see the look on his face, and I knew my suspicion was right. "Did you just buy all my prints? Yes or no Jacob, an easy question, honesty remember?"

"I love your work Jenna, I want your photo's, and it's a legitimate sale."

"No, it's not legitimate when you hide it under the disguise of a lie. After knowing me as long as you have, you still don't get how important honesty is for me? I feel like you don't have confidence in my work, so you have to come in and save the day. Jacob, I didn't care if I didn't get one offer, but I wanted it to be real now it's ..."

I just stopped talking and left him standing there. I walked back over to my prints and pulled all the sold tickets off of them. Everyone just looked at me, and I just shook my head and pointed to Jacob. They all smiled and walked away, expecting fireworks to soon explode. I told them I would be free at 11:00 if they wanted to meet for a late bite or drink, we could meet at the hotel a block down the street.

Jeff walked over to me to calm me down, I think. He made a point to tell me that Jacob sent my mom money for the ticket and paid for her room, so not to be too mad at him for trying to make my event a big success in every way.

That's new, Jeff standing up for Jacob, I hadn't said one word against Jacob, and everyone is running to his defense. Am I being unreasonable to want my husband to be honest with me? Am I such a terrible wife to expect mutual respect from my soul mate?

Never a dull moment, my feet are killing me and with all our family here, "for me," I feel obligated to spend time with them and entertain them. Then I had another sick thought pop into my head, and I went back over to Jacob, "another private word please."

He came over to me, looking down at his feet. "Jacob I really hope I'm wrong about this, but just tell me the truth, did you set up this whole Art in New York City opportunity up for me? Did you have anything to do with this, behind my back with my professor? Did you Jacob? Oh no Jacob, I can see it in your eyes." I had to lean against the wall. He did this, to me on purpose. "Why would you do this, why?"

"Jenna, I know you love photography and I thought this would be a special experience for you. Yes, I arranged it through your professor, but he agrees your work is good and worthy of gallery exposure. I did all this for you Jenna."

I could feel the strength fall out of my face. I could feel my cheeks sink down to my jaw bone. "Jacob how could you do this to me? Go behind my back and do this terrible thing to me? None of this is real, it's all one huge orchestrated lie directed by you. You bought my spot in here, and everyone is here to mock me?

I'm leaving. I can't believe you don't know me at all Jacob, I'm beyond crushed. To do this to me, to humiliate me like this, it was unnecessary and is so hurtful you know how I love lies, thanks Jacob. I can't even find the words. I'm walking to the hotel, and you can say my goodbye's to Dane, I'm sure he's been laughing at me for the last couple days. I need some space and air."

I walked over to my mom and told her in her ear what

had happened and to enjoy New York. Give Jeff my love, I'm out of here. I walked out alone, and Brandon followed me out the door. I didn't have the energy to fight him too.

He asked, "Jenna, are you okay?"

"No Brandon, I married an idiot, this whole exhibit, it was all a lie. Jacob paid to have my art here in this exhibit. I was an idiot, I thought this was as it appeared."

"Your work has really improved and some of them are really perfection. Don't let his over eagerness take away from your Art, you really are talented. Can I walk you to your destination?"

"Sure, I'm going back to my room."

He put his arm around me, and I just hooked my arm around his waist, and we walked slowly to my hotel. I leaned in under his arm, and we walked the block and a half together. We stopped for me to take off my heels, then he carried my shoes and we continued walking to the hotel.

I hugged him, no kissing at the hotel, just outside the doors. "I'm so sorry for this colossal waste of a trip to a fake Art exhibit".

"Seeing you again was never a waste of time or money".

"Thank you for being so kind. I'm going to my room. I'm sure Kourtney will be missing you by now."

"I'm sure she didn't even notice I was gone."

I just smiled and said, "Thanks Brandon, for being here to support me and again I'm so sorry for the lie." I turned and walked into the hotel before I broke down and bawled like a baby.

CHAPTER 9

Good Intentions Fallout

I cannot believe this, why did He do this? How can he not know me better than that? Why? Why would he do this to me? He's supposed to know me better than anyone else but he's clueless. I'm so embarrassed, humiliated, hurt and all of it was a lie created by Jacob. It serves no purpose, a waste of time energy and money. I turned around and Brandon was still standing there

I went back out and thanked Brandon again, hugged him and said thanks for coming Brandon; I hope you and Kourtney enjoy your time in New York while you're here. Then before he could say anything I would have to deal with, I turned again and walked inside my hotel entry through the lobby and to my elevator. I didn't want to be so self-absorbed that I wasn't kind to my old friend Brandon.

In my room, I took off my clothes, put on my swimsuit and walked down to the hotel pool and hot tub. I sat in the hot tub until I was so hot, I felt like I would pass out. Then I got into the cool pool and swam until I had no energy left.

Then I took a towel someone left on a chair and covered my wet body as I walked to the elevator then to my room. Darn, I forgot my key to get back into my room. I knocked on the door and Jacob answered it. He just opened the door. No words spoken.

I went to the bathroom to shower off the chlorine which was really strong in the pool. The chlorine made my eyes look bloodshot and my throat burned from breathing in all the hot tub chlorine fumes.

They burned and I just stood in the shower and cried and cried. It reminded me of when Jacob kicked me out of his life and I was empty and alone, crying my-self to sleep. A terrible time in my life, and here I am back to that same betrayed feeling again.

I got out of the shower took my towel to cover my body, and walked out covered up and walked over to my suit case. Not one non-sexy thing to wear to bed. I walked over to Jacob's suitcase and took one of his tee-shirts and went to the bathroom and put it on. It covered everything, nothing see-through, revealing or lacy tonight.

I came out and Jacob said, "you can make a tee shirt sexy." I just grinned; he didn't deserve a real smile. I crawled into bed curled up into a ball and planned on trying to go to sleep. I just wanted to forget this whole situation.

Jacob said, "a married couple should never go to bed mad."

I got out of bed and sat on the couch. He got up and followed. He said, "Jenna, I'm sorry. I didn't think you'd ever find out."

"Oh great, so now you think I'm too stupid to keep up with you. I'm not smart enough to catch you in a lie or lies? Nice to know you think so highly of me Jacob. This just keeps getting better. How do you think I feel knowing I was happy and content with learning and growing in my photography class and now, I'm a laughingstock.

I can't go back to class because of your actions! You

took something pure and honest and made it painful for me, one big lie. I don't understand why you would think I would want this recognition, attention that's not my thing.

But the lies, behind my back, deceptions, that is what has broken my heart." I could feel the tears lumping in the back of my throat and I refused to let them fall. They kept filling up in my eyes and I had to close my eyes.

"Jenna, looking at this in hindsight, I see what I did backfired on me. I work large deals at work all the time and thought you'd like this, a trip to New York, seeing your mom, sharing your pictures with the world. I just want to make your dreams come true. I have the power and resources to do it, and I did. I am sorry I over stepped my boundaries. But it was because I love you. I'm sorry I hurt you, that wasn't what I wanted at all."

"I know Jacob. Now that we've talked, can I please go to sleep? I'm so tired. I don't want to say anything I will regret, and I want to have a clear head to process all this if it's okay with you."

"Sure, if that's what you want, can I have a kiss goodnight?"

"I'm your wife, you can kiss me." He kissed me, and it was Jacob kissing me, but for the first time ever, it was just a kiss. I felt nothing for him, it was like I was kissing a stranger, I felt nothing. I just stood back and looked at him. The kiss more than anything, scared me. We have a problem, but I need sleep, this nightmare needs to end. I cannot process one more thing.

"Jacob, if you are going to be up for a while, would you mind canceling our tickets for the musicals Wicked and Chicago if it's possible to get your money back, and I'm fine to go home tomorrow if you are good with that."

"Are you sure, you were so excited to see Broadway shows. I'll do what you want me to do, but do you want me to wait until tomorrow and see how you feel then?"

"Sure Jacob, whatever you want to do. Good night."

I heard Jacob on the phone cancelling our reservations for the shows. He was capable of listening to me and following my requests. And I don't know what he did after that because I fell asleep.

I woke up and I was wrapped up in Jacob, and he in me and if felt wonderful. He meant well. Forgive and forget, that's what people who are in love do for each other.

"Jacob," I whispered as I was still on his chest and under his arm. "Jacob," I felt him stir, then said "Yes?"

"I love you, and I'm sorry if I did or said anything last night that would make you embarrassed to be my husband." A tear fell from my eye and fell down his chest. He pulled me away from him and sat straight up in bed.

"Jenna, you are going to make me turn in my man card, I'm so close to bawling like a baby. You tear my heart out when you cry, and when I'm the one who has caused you the pain, I regret my decisions and the pain and embarrassment I've caused you with all my good intentions.

I'm sorry I keep screwing up, but I've never loved someone so completely before, and this is all new to me. I wanted to do something special for you and I just should have stayed out of it and let you have your own success in your own time. I'm so sorry I hurt you."

"Jacob, you kissed me last night, and for the first time ever, I didn't feel anything for you or about you, or about your touch. It was like the connection between my lips and my heart had been broken."

Jacob jumped out of bed and stood looking out the window. He was running his hands through his hair and I just sat in the middle of the bed. "Oh God Jenna, how do I fix this?" He continued running his hands through his hair, and I was feeling like I was going to be sick.

"I don't know. I really don't know. Maybe kiss me again?" He rushed to my bed, kissed me and I felt the love, I felt the sorry, the fear, and the hopelessness. I stopped him.

"Jacob, stop. It's okay. I do love you, I feel your love, but don't ever risk what we have for a lie, any kind of lie, ever again! Do you get it Jacob? You will never win with a lie, NEVER! Not with me ever! Do you understand me? Is this clear for you now?"

"Yes. I love you, I'm so sorry. I screwed up". Then the kissing and making up took place.

I took a shower and got dressed, my feet hurt from wearing high heels yesterday. All that pretending and it was all for nothing. The more I think about it, the madder I get. What a waste of time and energy. I must quit thinking about this.

"When are we leaving?"

"Tonight at 4:00, we can stay here till noon, get something to eat and then get to the airport for departure."

I was thinking but didn't say, *all that time, energy, money for nothing, empty fake nothingness, but I don't want to hurt him with this over and over. I don't play games, you hurt me, so now I'll hurt you, never my style. I just needed to forgive and let my heart heal from the betrayal I had just experienced. I need some time to move on from this, I just want to leave this town and the memories.*

Jacob asked what I was thinking, so I told him. "I want you to be clear that I forgive you for this colossal lie. I'm deeply hurt and this one is going to take me some time to get over. I need time to heal. Now I don't need you to apologize over and over. I just need us to be honest and move forward."

"Are you hungry because I'm really hungry, how about eggs benedict? Let's go downstairs and eat." We went down stairs and Jacob's brothers and dad were all down there eating too, great timing for me. We sat with them and ate.

Andrew said, "Jacob it's a good thing she married you

because no other woman would put up with you and our family." I just shook my head no, and didn't say anything. Jacob's retort was "eat your food Andrew, I'm not the only one on thin ice, you should quit while you're ahead."

Andrew just smiled at me and drank his orange juice. I leaned over and whispered in Andrews' ear, "Andrew will it bother you if I order alcohol?"

He just laughed out loud and said, "Sweet Jenna, you can order a full case of alcohol it won't bother me."

"I usually don't drink, but I've heard mimosas are good and I've always wanted to try them, so I ordered a pitcher of mimosas. Once I tasted how delicious they were, I asked our waitress to keep them coming. I had four drinks, more than Jacob had ever seen me drink before (more than I'd ever drunk in my life especially at one time). Jacob was just quiet and visiting with his family. I just ate and drank.

I listened to their excitement for New York and the list of places they wanted to see. I remember that excitement and love when we first got here. I told them about the night club we went to that was so much fun, about the bridge and ferry and the girlfriends were excited to hear about where to get the best deals on the outside vendors. It sounded like they would have a great time here. I was glad it wouldn't be a totally wasted visit for them.

I warned them about the Prada bag vendor who had me walk through a secret door behind a wall of purses to find really nice items. It was sort of scary once I was behind the wall, they had rows and rows of women in an upstairs room that was like a scene from a movie all sewing on machines, and I had no idea this tiny shop had this big room behind this door.

Then I was afraid I would be kidnapped, and Jacob wouldn't know where I was. I told them my husband had my money and I needed to get my money and they walked me back out. So, I told on myself to make sure the girls wouldn't make the same stupid mistake for a "real Prada product".

This was the first time Jacob was hearing this story and he was just sitting there at the table shaking his head like he couldn't believe I'd do something so stupid. It was unwise, but mimosas made me say more than I needed to say. But if I can forgive him for ill-advised choices, he should be able to forgive me.

The brothers and girlfriends invited us to go with them. Before Jacob could speak for us, I said we were headed back early. But I thanked them for the invitation. "Before everyone leaves, I just wanted to say thank you for coming, even though it didn't end up being exactly what we expected, sometimes we get thrown a curve ball. It's just nice to know that I have family that's there for me. Thank you everyone". The guys just smiled the girls just looked at the men like they didn't know how to respond.

I said, "It's just a thank you no response is required ladies so just relax and enjoy your trip." Then I motioned for our waiter to bring me another pitcher of mimosas, they were so good I couldn't get enough.

I was relaxed and chilling. A big change from yesterday, today was already much better and getting better by the minute. I should have had a pitcher of mimosas last night and things might have been entirely different today, who knows? Who am I kidding? I don't turn to alcohol to solve my problems. I'm not thinking clearly. I need to be alone and get myself in-line

CHAPTER 10

What's Next?

I was buzzed and feeling no pain and Jacob, was quiet actually silent with me. His family was leaving to go explore New York City, and we were going back upstairs to get our stuff to go to the airport. I didn't need to be all serious and upset.

Jacob was with me he would take care of everything. He just wanted a pretty girl on his arm, not a woman who thinks or has... stop it Jenna. He's your husband and he loves you, so quit pouting, and move on.

We got back to our room and Jacob said, "Jenna, talk it out, don't drink, it's not you; you've never had four drinks in a row before, have you?"

I just looked at him and said "Nope."

"Then why now?"

"I'm sorry Jacob, did I embarrass you in front of your family? I didn't mean to, I just really like the taste of mimosas and just got carried away. How many did I have?"

"You didn't embarrass me, but if you are playing that

game, that's fine I deserve it."

"Game" Are you kidding me? You think you hurt me so I'm going to act five years old and hurt you back? Who are you? You don't know me at all Jacob."

I stormed into the bathroom and locked the door. I couldn't be near him. He's a stranger and I can't think. I've trusted him with my deepest thoughts, dreams, heart and future, and what? He thinks I'm playing games because I relax with a few drinks for the first time in my life.

I can't do anything right in his eyes. I'm not smart enough to figure out he's telling me lies, and now I'm a lush too? A relationship takes two to make it work, and he has no idea of who I am or how I think. I'm supposed to forgive him, but I can't have four harmless drinks. I need space to think, space away from Jacob, so I can see things clearly, and honestly.

"Jenna, damn it, I didn't mean it."

"Yes, you did, you said it, so you thought it. Be honest, is it that hard for you to just tell me the truth, tell yourself the truth? I'm taking a Jacuzzi. Do you need to use the room before I get into the tub?"

"Yes, let me in."

I unlocked the door and he said, "Jenna you've been drinking a lot and you didn't eat very much. Please don't lock the door and get in a hot tub. Please just leave the door unlocked so if you need me, I could get to you."

I started taking off my clothes and singing a song stuck in my head from the elevator. "Jacob are you joining me?"

"No, I'll sit out here and enjoy the show."

"Fine but shut the door you are letting the cold air in here." So I put bubbles across my private parts and stood up in the tub and started dancing and singing. Jacob was sitting on the stool just laughing his sides off.

It was worth making a fool out of myself to see him on the floor laughing. "I'm not drunk, I'm just chilling out before I go home sweetheart." Jacob got up and said, "You need to sit down before you slip and fall and break an ankle again."

Totally a possibility, so I sat down, in the warm bubbling water and Jacob, brought me a bottle of water and told me I would need to hydrate before we flew home. I did as I was told. Jacob left the bathroom and checked the room to make sure we had everything packed.

He asked, "Jenna, are you doing okay in there?" No response. He got up and saw through the mirror that I my eyes were closed and I was slowly sliding under the water. When I woke up, I was in bed and Jacob was yelling at me.

I pushed him out of my face and realized that my whole left side hurt like I'd been drug across the room and jumped on top of with a car. "

"Why am I in bed?"

"Because you drank too much, got in the hot tub and you passed out. You were going under the water when I grabbed you and carried you to the bed."

"Did I hit something because my jaw really hurts, what did I do to my jaw?"

"I may have smacked you harder than I meant to when I was trying to get you to wake up. You scared me!" He ran his fingers through his hair and said in a low strong tone, "You are full time drama. You require round the clock care, you really do, it's exhausting!"

"Translation I'm needy? No that's not me, and not going to be me! Jacob, I will be fine, and I'll never put you in that position again. So you don't have to worry about me being a drain on you full time for care! Don't we have a plane to catch?"

I sat up immediately and put my clothes on and pulled my luggage to the door. I was mad at myself for drinking more than I have ever in my life, in front of his family and then passing out in a tub full of water. I know better than that. What was wrong with me? This was self-destructive behavior, and it was not a healthy way to deal with my problems and with Jacob.

"I was just scared you could have died. I was upset."

"Sorry I put you in that position, it won't happen again. Are you ready to go?"

Jacob looked like he'd been run through a ringer. "I'm right behind you, just hold the elevator for me." Then I suddenly had a great idea. I held the elevator door for Jacob until he was almost there, and then at the last minute, I let the door slide shut right before he could actually touch the door. Then I made eye contact with him, and just as I was looking at his shocked face of me letting the door slam in his face, I purposefully bit my bottom lip and the doors closed. He saw me then boom the door shut.

I laughed all the way down to the first-floor lobby. I was laughing when I got off the elevator and still laughing when he got off the next elevator and walked up behind me and smacked my butt. I liked it when he was being playful, not so serious. I turned around to face him, and he was grinning and shaking his head no.

I just reached around, grabbed his hair, pulled it and we were kissing passionately in the lobby of the hotel. He was such a no public display of affection at home, but he's getting freer to be responsive the longer we are together. "Jacob let's not fight. You hurt me deeply but I still love you. I hope if I'm able to forgive you and forget that you can do the same for me."

"Jenna, I'm sorry and no more lip biting! You know what I've told you about that."

"Yes, I do, and that's exactly why I laughed for the next five minutes coming down the elevator and waiting for you to get down here too. It was too funny to hold inside and I'd do it again, that's the kind of woman you married."

Jacob checked us out of the hotel, and we were in a taxi on the way to the airport. Jacob said, "So how was it seeing Brandon yesterday?" I couldn't believe he brought up Brandon.

"Well Jacob, it must have been better for you than me, because he's not even a distant thought in my mind today, but he's the first serious conversation you want to have with me after yesterday? Maybe it isn't just one of us in this relationship that's how did you put it, oh yeah, full time care."

"I didn't mean to make you mad. I just wanted to have the conversation, to know how you felt, what you were thinking. You know communicate like you said you wanted."

"Okay Jacob, we'll have this talk now if that's what you want. It was great to see Brandon and his beautiful daughter. He is a great friend and I hate that I called him and invited him back into this circus of a life I live.

He spent his hard-earned money and brought his daughter to make me feel special and supported. He walked me back to the hotel and was kind as always and told me how he honestly felt. He said I could always come back that he'd be there for me with open arms."

"What did you say to that?"

"How's next Saturday, work for you Brandon?"

"What?"

"What do you think I told him? I told him thanks that meant a lot to me, but I was married till death did us part. And I may want to kill you sometimes, like last night, but at the end of the day, I still love you, you, big idiot husband of mine. I told him he needed to move on and find someone to share his nights and kisses with, because he was always a great kisser."

"Okay, I don't want to know any more, sorry I asked."

"Then don't ask Jacob. You know I'm honest, so think about who I am, and how I respond to things. I'm pretty predictable about how I feel about things. I may not say or do what you want me to do and say, but you will never have to second guess situations and if they are real or not. I am just as I seem, no game playing, manipulating, or lying.

Sometimes I think you know me better than anyone ever has ever, and other times it's like you don't have a clue of who I am at all. It's so hurtful to think the man I love with my hopes and dreams acts like I'm a total stranger and you don't have a clue of who I am, or what's important to me (truth/honesty a deal breaker).

I think I'm pretty easy to figure out, even sort of boring, but that's the part that hurts the most. It's never going to be another man that would ever break us up; it will be you not trusting me, or your lies. That's the stuff that separates the heart and heat of a couple.

Do you get it Jacob, the truth is the only way for us to work? I hope you figure it out, before it's too late for us. I've been very clear about the truth and a deal breaker status even before our "first-second date."

"Is that a threat?"

"Brilliant, once again, you don't have a clue of whom I am to even ask that question just proves you don't know me at all. Have I ever threatened you, ever? Did you not just hear what I said to you? Stop talking to me. Every time you open your mouth you are stabbing my heart. I can't take one more word from you, not a word. If you really feel the things you are sayings to me then you've ended us before we even had a chance to bloom and grow. (My eyes start filling up with tears, and he said my name)

"Jenna..."

"Please Jacob, listen to my plea, not a word, I'm going to break down and ball like a baby then you will feel bad because I'm crying. I just looked at him like I was hurt, What Jacob? What do you want to say now?"

"Jenna, I love you and I'm sorry. That seems to be the only thing I can say that doesn't get you defensive and mad at me."

"Yes Jacob, the problem is all me and my reactions. Nice name calling Jacob, so far. I'm defensive, mad, full time care, I think I've been a good listener to what you've been saying to me and about me and I don't think I missed anything. I didn't look, listen, or speak another word to Jacob at the airport or on the plane.

Chapter 11

Up in the Air

I sat next to a businessman on the plane, and he flirted with me. I didn't stop him. He asked me to go out when we landed, but I told him, I couldn't because I have a ring and a man attached to that ring, but we are on shaky ground. Then he told me maybe I should get your number in case things change. I told him I don't give out my number, but I'll take yours, in case, I didn't want to be rude, and he gave me his business card and I put it in my purse.

The plane landed and I walked off without saying a word to Jacob. I got my carry-on bag and walked to the luggage return. Then I picked up my own luggage off the carousal and walked out to our car. I had the key in my purse so I loaded my luggage and Jacob just stood there.

"Can I ride home with you?"

"Sure hop in." He put his luggage into the back and walked around to the driver's seat.

"Do you mind if I drive? Thanks, are you hungry, we

could stop somewhere and get something before we go home?"

"No."

Then he said "Jenna, you had a lot to drink today, barely ate any food, passed out and nearly died, and flirted with another man in front of me for a solid hour (not that you play games), so me being the husband who can't do or say anything right, just wanted you to eat something before you get so hungry that you get sick. We are going to stop somewhere. What do you want to eat?"

"I don't care, whatever you want. There's a Mexican restaurant up ahead, does that sound good to you?"

"Sure, it sounds good to me." Next thing I knew we were inside and eating chips and cheese dip. I love cheese; it's a soothing food for me. I had water to drink with my food and I really was hungrier than I thought I was. We ate, no talking. Then back to the car to go home. We got home and before we got out of the car I had to say something, the silence between us was deafening.

"I was wrong to let that man flirt with me and I didn't stop him. I'm sorry. I could have just told him you were my husband and he would have stopped, but you didn't say anything to that man either. You hurt me and our relationship by your words and actions and I just didn't want to talk and do any more damage.

If you think about the plane ride, he was the one who did all the talking and I did not give him my phone or my phone number or encourage him. I told him I was married if you remember. I politely took his business card, which I threw away already.

You hurt me, but I wasn't trying to hurt you back, to make you pay. That's not me, can't you see it in my eyes; hear it in my hearts cry? I just didn't want to talk to you at that moment. I just wanted to ignore our situation for some time to think. I don't want to hurt you intentionally or unintentionally honestly. I think that's what I was thinking when I put us in that uncomfortable situation, so again I'm sorry.

I love you and we just keep hurting one another. Why do we keep doing this to each other? Do you think we should take a break from each other for a while to figure this out? I can't go back to my photography class ever again.

I feel like a fool when I even think of taking pictures now and I can't find a teaching job here, and you feel like you need to create a pretend world to make me happy apparently. Maybe we need to step back and rethink what we are doing to each other and why we are in this downhill spin. I want to fix this, but don't know where to start. What do you think we should do?"

"You want a divorce?"

"No Jacob, you don't hear what I'm saying, I said a break to think. I never said divorce. Why, do you want to divorce me?"

"I don't know."

"You don't know?" Wow, well clearly, we do need a break so you can figure out what you do want maybe that's part of our problem. A husband should know if he wants his wife. And a wife should know if she wants her husband. We were silent for a while. Then I finally spoke, Jacob if you want me to leave you, if you're not sure you love me anymore, then I'll take the truck and leave in the morning. I'll do that if that's what you want."

"If that's what you want Jenna." We made it home. I just got out of the car. I left my luggage in the car, I went inside got my camera and lenses and took them out to the car. One less thing I'll have to pack in the morning.

Then I took everything that I had added or changed to his place since I'd been there, which wasn't a lot, and moved all that stuff into my photography room. Hum, my photography room was going to be a nursery, but our baby died, then my photography room and that dream was dead now too.

I just shut the door to "My dead space" in his house that way Jacob wouldn't have to see anything to make him think of me. His house all back to himself. I got my pet carriers and put them in the car so they would be ready for Molly and Moose in the morning. My heart was hurting so bad I knew I wouldn't sleep tonight, so I just got my dogs, put them in the car then went in to say goodbye to Jacob.

Jacob was sitting at the table and had a diet dr. pepper out waiting for me. I saw it and came up from behind him and just hugged his neck and thanked him. He didn't turn toward me or move in any way to show me any affection, so I let him go. Jacob said, "I see you are cleaning house."

"I thought you wanted a break from me, so I moved all my stuff that I got to change your place to make it our place. I moved things into the photography room so you wouldn't have to see it and think of me. I don't want to hurt you Jacob. I was just trying to think of you and your feelings and your needs."

"You think out of sight will be out of mind?"

"I don't know Jacob, will it? (No answer.) I just wanted to make this easier on you. I'm sure I didn't do the right thing once again; I don't seem to be able to do or say anything right to please you and that breaks my heart. I don't know what to do for us. That's why I thought a break would give us perspective to see things clearly without hurting each other. I don't know what to do or say to fix this. What do you think Jacob? What are you feeling?"

"You all packed, the dogs in the car?"

"Yes."

"You are leaving now?"

"I don't know, I didn't feel tired before, but now I feel exhausted."

"Well, I'm sure you will get your energy back in a few minutes, you should just go Jenna, if you are going just go. Remember like a Band-Aid, do it quickly less painful that way."

"Jacob what are we doing? I love you. I want us to work, I just want us to work better that's all I was trying to say or suggest to you."

"No Jenna, you were right, we need a break, so I'll give you a break. Is it still going to be a six months separation?"

"Jacob, I was thinking a few days to clear our minds, not half a year. Do you want me to be gone, out of your life for six months?" He didn't say anything.

"Why are you so mad at me?"

"I don't know Jenna; I guess I need a break to figure it out."

"Jacob, I feel like this is goodbye and I don't want that, I love you Jacob. I'm sorry for hurting you honestly, I'm so sorry. I want us to work."

"Jenna, we need a break to see if we have anything worth saving. "

"To see if we have anything worth saving. I can't make you love me. Okay, you need time. Can I kiss you, goodbye?" He just gave me a look like he was doing me a favor and we kissed. But it wasn't a loving kiss. It was hurtful.

He was squeezing my butt and not any affection, no love, it was cold and cruel. It broke my heart to be treated with no affection from him, just another way to break my heart. I may have just lost the man I loved, and I can't believe it. I had to turn away from him. I got my voice steady.

"Thank you for the Diet Dr. Pepper," and walked out of the door. I had a difficult time getting my key into the ignition, but finally blinked the tears away enough to get my car started. I held my tears from flowing until I was in the car and driving out of his driveway.

Here he is again, throwing me away, and this time I behaved badly, flirting with another man. I thought my suggestion to take a break would be a positive thing, not an end our marriage thing.

He thinks I'm full time needy. But he did just have to save my life physically, but he rips my heart out with his unkind words and actions. I'm devastated.

I put my car back into park and got out of my car and ran back to the porch where Jacob was sitting. "Please Jacob, let's not do this. We've both done and said hurtful things this weekend, I love you, let's not separate.

Let me stay with you. We can work this out, but you have to want me to stay. What do you want? Please talk with me; let's work this out together I don't want to be away from you for six months."

"I really think you should hit the road before it rains, it looks like we could get a bad storm." What good would it do to stay if that's what he's thinking and how he's feeling? He didn't respond with "No don't go Jenna, I'm sorry Jenna. No don't go Jenna, I love you too."

He didn't say anything hopeful, it was cold, and not how you would ever treat someone you loved. He doesn't love me. He wanted me to leave for six months. Don't beg Jenna, just leave. I'm gone, I can't stay with that attitude and behavior. He left me no choice.

I shook my head and said, "Okay Jacob, goodbye." I got back in the car started it and turned around and headed for Missouri. I didn't get twenty-five miles down the road when it started raining so hard, I couldn't see a car link in front of me.

I was crying and slowing down so I could see the road and the next thing I know, the emergency medical technician asked me for a name to contact in an emergency. I told them Andrew Jamison, because I knew he was closer to get to me than my brother.

When I became alert enough to talk, it was the next day, and I was in a hospital room. Andrew was sitting by my bedside.

CHAPTER 12

Wrecked

"Andrew what just happened to me?"

"You were hit broadsided by a truck. It was raining hard and the other car was going too fast and was hydroplaning and hit you. Your car is totaled Jenna, I'm so sorry."

"My dogs Andrew, are my dogs okay?"

"I'm sorry Jenna, they didn't make it. I started crying, it's all my fault it was raining I couldn't see, I was crying, they're dead."

"Why did you give them my name and not Jacob's?"

"Andrew you cannot tell Jacob I'm here, he threw me out again and told me he doesn't want to hear from me for six months."

"Jenna, you can't be serious, you hit your head you have a concussion."

"I wish I'd been killed, and I wouldn't have this broken heart. I cannot believe he keeps doing this to me; I can't do this again Andrew. I love that idiot, but my dogs are dead because he threw me away again. I could have died too, and he wouldn't let me stay the night. I practically begged him to reconsider, to let me stay with him, but you can't make someone love you when they don't anymore.

I have nothing and no one and I needed a friend, so I gave them your name. They asked me my next of kin and I couldn't say Jacob, so I just thought of you. I don't have a car, what am I going to do? I need help to think clearly, my head is killing me."

"Jenna, let me get a nurse to get you something for your headache then we can talk."

"Wait a minute Andrew, how did you get here? You were in New York."

"Jenna, I came as soon as they called me. You've been out for a day. I got in last night."

"Thank you for being here for me, you are a good brother." He just let me sit up and cry on his shoulder until I fell back to sleep. When I woke up, Jacob was sitting on the end of my bed. I thought I was seeing things. Jacob just looked at me and said, "Jenna, was your wreck an accident or did you do this on purpose so I would come back to you?"

Andrew was in the room when he said this to me, I said, "Jacob my car is totaled, my dogs are dead, my body is broken, and I did all that so I could see you sit at the end of my bed and accuse me of who knows what. I asked Andrew not to tell you I was here!"

"He didn't, it was on the police radio, and it sounded like your car, so I called to find out and heard it was you, so I came to see if you are okay.

I ignored him for a moment and said "Andrew, I'm sorry, I knew I could trust you, that's why I gave them your name as my contact." Jacob spoke up again, not happy that I wasn't giving him my full attention, so Jenna, did you try to kill yourself because you couldn't have me?

I was doing all I could do not to cry. I couldn't look at

Jacob in the face. I couldn't even comment on Jacob's cruel comment. I looked at Andrew and was so glad he was here and hearing what Jacob was saying to me. I had to change the subject before I lost my composure. "Andrew would you please find Molly and Moose and make sure they get a proper burial? Please? "

"Jenna, I'll make sure they are taken care of, I know you loved your fur balls, I liked them too."

"Thank you, that would make me feel so much better knowing they are laid to rest. Thank you!"

Jacob just walked over and took my hand. "Jenna, are you okay?" I had to look at him to answer him. "I don't know, what did the doctor say?"

"You broke your left leg and left arm when the car hit you. You have other minor bruising and swelling and bruised your kidneys, but you should be fine. Thank goodness you had your seatbelt on, or you would have been dead."

"Jacob you have to know that I did not try to kill myself, or my dogs, or destroy my new car. That is not who I am. Once again, your words hurt me worse than any broken bones ever could. Do you really think I would kill my dogs to make you call me? What has happened to us? How did I lose your trust? How could I be such a stranger to you?"

"I don't think you ever had my trust. I've tried to trust you over and over and I keep going back to not trusting you."

"Why, what did I do to make you not trust me, please tell me Jacob, I'm desperate to know what I did?"

"I don't know, I just think you are hiding something from me, and I can't think straight."

How do I keep attracting these men who don't know me and break my heart? "Jacob if we don't have trust, we don't have a relationship we don't have anything. Honesty and trust go hand in hand. We are officially over.

Just send me divorce papers and you won't have to

worry about me trying to trick you or get you to call me ever again. I'm out of your life forever! You won't have to worry or think about me ever again. I've survived you throwing me away once before and I will learn to survive this too.

I will always wish you the best and I will miss the "us" that could have been. The "Us" that's lived in my mind and heart from the day I first saw you walk into your Grandma Ruth's parlor. I wish you the best Jacob, I will miss you.

But I can't do this with you ever again. It will not only break my heart but literally kill me. There will be no next time. Do you have any feelings for me at all; any feeling for me as your wife? Do you feel anything Jacob?"

"Jenna, can I kiss you, goodbye?"

"No Jacob, we did that earlier tonight at your house, no I guess that was yesterday, sorry. I didn't do any of this on purpose to get you to call me Jacob or kiss me or for you to come by to see me in the hospital, so no kissing. I reached out to you, I begged you to let me stay to work it out and once again you tossed me out of your house.

Sorry you found out I was hurt. Just send me the divorce papers and I'll sign them Jacob. If you could please get my car fixed as soon as possible that's all I'll ask from you. Then I can get out of Kentucky, and you will never ever have to see or hear from me again. Not in six months, not ever. Jacob please leave; quickly, remember like a Band-Aid isn't that what you told me."

"Jenna, I'm kissing you, goodbye. He came over and kissed me like he loved me, but his words and his actions once again don't support the physical response our bodies give to one another. Jenna what are we doing?"

"Once again you threw me away. We didn't learn anything from the last time we were separated. You are doing it to us again and once again I don't understand why. I'm the only one broken. Each time you make me leave you, it kills a part of my heart that I never really ever get full use again. I really don't think I would live through a third kick her to the curb scenario from you. Please go."

"Jenna don't…. I'm sorry, just stay we can work things out."

"Jacob, I'm really tired you should leave."

"I'll be back to see you tomorrow."

Jacob left and I called Brandon and told him everything that I could remember that had happened since New York. He said he was so sorry about Molly and Moose. And he would be here for me if I wanted him to be here.

I told him that if he would come in three days that would give me time to recover a little and then when they dismissed me from the hospital Brandon could bring me home. It would help me sleep, knowing I was going to be okay and with someone safe.

"Jenna, Jacob's a fool. I will never throw you away. I know what that feels like and I would never do that to you."

"Brandon, I realize that Jacob is a lot to deal with and if you don't want to have to possibly deal with him, I won't blame you if you don't want to come and get me. I'll call my brother to come and get me.

There is no pressure, I just thought of you, and I'm broken. I'm literally a broken woman, and if you don't want to have anything to do with me, I totally understand. Do you need time to think? Should I just call my brother?"

"No, tell me your room number and I'll keep in contact with you and if your plans change, I can be flexible. I'll be there in three days unless I hear differently from you."

"Thank you for letting me depend on you, I'll talk to you soon."

I went to sleep and when I woke up, I had a beautiful flower arrangement in my room from Brandon. He's so thoughtful. It helps take away that hospital smell from my room and I loved the beautiful arrangements. Andrew was at the foot of my bed and so was Eddie. "Hi guys, Andrew did you find my dogs?"

"Yes, they are resting in peace now. They had happy lives, you loved them, and they loved you."

"Thank you for being here for me, like a true brother, I appreciate you I really do. Hey steady Eddie, what are you doing here?"

"I came to check on you as soon as we landed from our New York trip. What happened Jenna, you look awful, and you never look awful?"

"Well Jacob kicked me out, said not to call him for six months, and I begged to stay, for him to forgive me for everything I did, and he just said I should go. So, after begging to stay, I had no choice, I drove in the rain, crying, and I couldn't see well, and then something hit me, and that's all I remember.

I do remember them asking me who my emergency contact was, and I said Andrew. I'm sorry I put you on the spot like that, but I needed a friend, and my husband didn't want to hear from me, I had, I have no one" (my eyes were filling up with tears and I was working at blinking to get them to go. I didn't want to be the poor cry baby).

"Jacob, showed up at my hospital room and wanted to know if I had the car accident on purpose so I could see him again. Can you see what I'm dealing with? He has no idea who I am, and as much as I loved him, I can't give my heart and life to a man who doesn't know or trust me. My broken bones will heal, but my heart will always wear the two fatal scars that ended our relationship.

Boys I'm sorry I couldn't stay and be your sister. But I was married to crazy before and I won't give away another 10 years of my life hoping and praying he will get better, that he will love me and trust me somehow, someway. I've been there and done that, and I can't live those same mistakes again. I have to go back to Missouri, my old house, my old safe life."

"Jenna, we love you and we will miss the music you put back in our lives."

"Thanks guys! If you are ever in Missouri, please call me and I'd love to see you and see who you eventually find to share your love and lives with. I will always wish you all the best. I hope you will remember the real me and not the version of me you may hear from someone else. Take good care of Jacob boys, he loves you." I heard familiar boots walking in the hall. I got quiet and grabbed my pillow almost fearful of what I was going to face today when Jacob walked back into my room.

"Hey boys do you mind giving my wife and me a few private minutes." Andrew said he would go down to the cafeteria would I like anything?

"Yes, I would love a Diet Dr. Pepper and Cheetos please." He walked up to my bed and kissed me on the head. How sweet to show that he cares about me in front of Jacob. Then Eddie came gave me a kiss on the lips and said "I hope I find someone as great as you one day Jenna. I would consider myself a lucky man."

"Eddie you are wonderful and if I was a few years younger," wink, wink. He just smiled and said, "good-bye Jenna Jamison."

I got tears in my eyes thinking of how hard I worked to get to know these guys and to be accepted and a part of the family. And now to feel the heart wrenching pain from being ripped away from my happy marriage, my husband, my life. Jacob was in the room, so I needed to stop the tears, he'll think I'm acting.

"Now Jacob, what can I do for you?"

"How are you feeling today?"

"Well, I got up to go to the bathroom by myself this morning and I'm sore, but I'll heal fine. You know me, I heal relatively quickly."

"Jenna, I'm sorry for everything I said and did. I don't know how I could think those terrible things about you much less say those things out loud to you. I'm so sorry."

"Jacob, are you saying you want me to stay now and not go? What happened to stay away for six months, you wanted to think, and now my dogs are dead, my car crashed, my bones broken and you've decided to give me another chance? Why did you want me to leave Jacob?"

"I don't know, Jenna, you just overwhelm me, and I can't think. It's like brain, emotional, and physical are on overload, you are just too much. I can't take you anymore, you just overwhelm me. That is the truth Jenna. It's not pretty but it's the way I feel, overwhelmed."

"If you will go see a counselor to get help dealing with your emotions then I'll gladly stay with you. I'll go to a marriage counselor with you, if your doctor thinks that will help us. But Jacob, you have to promise me that you will get professional help for me to be able to stay with you. If you are willing to do that, then I will stay and work on our future together."

"I don't need a doctor, I'm fine. You just frustrate me and I need time and space away from you. That's very normal and every couple goes through ups and downs."

"Jacob, it's not normal to kick your tired wife out in the rain when she's crying and begging to stay. That's not normal. I want to live honestly, not walking on egg shells in my own home. I've lived that life before and I don't want that life again. I can't do it no matter how much I love you."

"It's all drama with you, just relax, I'll sign the papers for you to get out of here and take you home. You hit your head you're not thinking clearly."

"Jacob, I'm serious, if you are not going to get professional mental help, then I'm not going home with you."

"Don't put this all on me. I'm not crazy you can't ask me to do this. Don't give me an ultimatum Jenna, you won't like my answer."

"I loved you and wanted to trust you but for that to happen, you need professional help. I can't stay; one day you love me, the next you don't, you do, you don't, stay, go. That isn't healthy for either of us and I can't live like a yo-yo. I'm a person with feelings, not a possession, a disposable thing.

I have never loved anyone more than I love you. I hope that one day my heart and your heart can mend from the intense fire that burnt in us for each other. I believe I will always have a part in my soul that will always hold the memories of us forever. Your decision to not get help is an ultimatum for me to leave."

"Jenna, you are on pain medications, and you are talking crazy, we will be fine."

I could see we were not making any progress, so I had to change the subject before I lost my mind. "Jacob did you find out anything about my truck? Can they fix it or what are my options?"

"I saw your truck and I have all the stuff out of the truck, your clothes, camera stuff, but your truck was totaled. The insurance policy is full coverage, so we can get the same car, they will be sending a check this week so when you get out of the hospital, we can get you a car. If you want a different color, we can do that too, whatever you want."

"Thanks for checking on all that for me Jacob, I appreciate it."

"Did you see where Andrew laid to rest Molly and Moose?"

"No, I didn't. I'm sorry about them too, they were cute dogs."

"Thanks, you don't need to sit here with me, I'm fine. I'm sure you have work to do. You don't need to worry about me Jacob, I'll be fine."

"You don't want your husband here with you?"

"If you are going to get help, then you can stay. If you

aren't going to get help then you need to leave because we can't fix this on our own. Like you told me yesterday and the day before that, do it quickly like a Band-Aide. You tell me, what are we doing?"

"Jenna, I honestly don't know what I should do. Can I have a day to think about it?"

"If you loved me and wanted us to have a future together then you will get help. If you want me to go, just say you aren't willing to get help. But take the day if you need it, it's a big decision. Thank you for considering this for us Jacob."

Jacob left and I asked the nurse to put a do not disturb sign on my door for visitor until I got off the phone. She said sure. I called attorney Sonny Strausz and asked if he could come to my hospital room. I need divorce papers and whatever else goes along with that. Sonny said he'd be up to see me in about an hour, two at tops.

I know if Jacob would have said "Jenna, I'll see a counselor" then it would be a no brainer, I'd stay and work on our marriage. But I got Jacob's answer "can I have a day to think about if we are worth me seeing a doctor."

Just in case he's not willing to fight for us, I want to have the paperwork ready to end this torture. Thank God my house didn't sell, but I gave most all my possessions away. My car insurance should have a check to buy a replacement, but I gave up my income, my career and now I have nothing.

I took a leave without pay, so I guess I could go to the school district office and see what I need to do to reinstate my leave papers. Maybe I can get some income and a teaching job or substitute teaching job for the rest of the year. I need to be logical, be practical, because if I think about all of this, my heart will burst and I'll lose my mind and my heart forever. I feel like I'm on the edge of a cliff and its foggy and rainy outside and I'm close to the slippery slope.

I need to be careful, sit still and let the fog lift and the rain subside so I don't end tragically. I called the nurse and asked her if anyone tried to get into my room while I was on the phone, she said no but Andrew was coming down the hall now, so he'd take off the privacy sign and help him into my room.

I was so ready for my pop and chips. "Thank you so much Andrew!" I told him about Jacob, and my conversation and he just shook his head.

"Jenna, I think you are right, he needs mental help if he has to stop and think about if his marriage is worth the work."

"Andrew, I don't want to put you in an uncomfortable position, so if you need to go, I will understand. But if you are okay to do this, would you just hug me for a minute. I lost my dogs, my car, broke bones, and am losing the love of my life and my best friend. I'm not trying to come on to you, you are my brother, and I just need to feel loved because I'm dying inside."

He came to the right side of my bed that didn't have a broken arm and leg casts on, and hugged me strongly yet gentle and I just melted in to his strength. I felt his warmth and I needed his help to get me through the pain.

"If you want to stay here for a while, you are welcome to stay with me at my place. It's an option for you if you want it. And it could be a private stay or tell everyone, I wouldn't care. I'm here for you. Do you want me to call your brother and fill him in on what's going on with you?"

"Not until I have Jacob's decision tomorrow. If Jacob decides to get help, then I don't want my family to know about this nightmare. But if he doesn't choose me or us, then I would love for you to please call Jeff and tell him everything for me. That would help me greatly. If I don't have to say it out loud then maybe it won't hurt so badly."

"Okay, what time do you want me to be here tomorrow?"

"If you are available, I would love you to be here when Jacob comes that way you will know if you should call Jeff. I think I forgot to thank you for the pop and chips, but most of all, thanks for just being here, being you, listening to my fears and reassuring me with the hugs. Thank you, Andrew, I mean it."

"My Dr. Pepper and chips are gone, and I would love a walk down the hall, but I need some clothes. Jacob says he has all my stuff they were all packed in my car when I was leaving, so he's got them all back at his place.

I need sweats, something I can slip over my arm and leg cast. I don't know where my purse is, or my money, credit cards any of that stuff is, but if you could check in the gift shop and see if they are selling any clothes that do not show your butt off with an open gown, I'd appreciate you buying me clothes."

"Sure, any color preference?"

"No, just big enough to get over my huge arm and leg casts. Keep track of what I owe you and I will pay you back when I find my purse."

"We are family, don't worry, I'll be back." I closed my eyes and must have fallen asleep, but the doctor came in and wanted to know how I was feeling. I told him physically fine but emotionally heart broken. I asked him when he would release me to go home and he said it could be as early as tomorrow. He said we were just waiting for my blood pressure to come up and stay at a healthy rate and that I needed to have a bowel movement, then he'd release me. Jenna, you need to eat and drink lots of water.

"Okay I'll eat. My brother-in-law went to get me some clothes. I want to do some walking in the halls for some exercise so my bowels will start moving and I'll eat. Thanks for taking good care of me doctor." Then there was a knock on my door, and it was my attorney.

The doctor left and I knew I was on the clock with Sonny. I told him I loved Jacob, and that I would know tomorrow if he was going to get professional help, or if he was going to throw us away. I don't want his money, I wanted him, but he never believed me. So I have plans to move back to Missouri if he decides not to see a counselor. But Sonny, what do I need to do?"

"Jenna, Jacob is worth millions, he has banks full of money; you will never have to work again. It would be nothing for him to give you a generous settlement."

"No Sonny, it's never been about his money. I will struggle financially and go without before I'll ever ask Jacob, for money. That's not who I am, never has been and never will be. I don't want him to ever think that I was with him for his money and with him not thinking clearly, I would rather go hungry and live on the streets than leave him with the thought that I just wanted his money.

I want him to know that with all his crazy times, I loved him for him. I know that's stupid but I love him and don't want to do anything that would hurt him. The only reason for this divorce is to motivate him to get the help he needs. I hope with my whole heart that he chooses me and us and gets the counseling he needs. Then your services won't be needed. But if not...."

"Good for you Jenna, as long as you have the money to pay me, then I'll do what you need."

"I just need a quick divorce if he won't get counseling. That's all I want." I'll call you tomorrow and let you know what Jacob decided for us. Thank you for coming and helping me with this situation, I will leave all the legal worry to you and remember I'm limited on funds so please do your best for me with that in mind."

Andrew came into the room. "How much of that did you hear?"

"Jenna, I heard it all. I was in the hall when he walked in. You are wrong, you need money, don't be stupid. Jacob has it, if he was thinking clearly; he'd make sure you were taken care of financially forever. You have to pay your bills."

"No, I want Jacob to know it was him I loved, not his money. I don't want him to ever confuse the two. He has enough confusion to deal with Andrew. I don't want to ever add to his problems, I want to help him, and love him. I wanted him to want me, to want us.

He wants me one minute and acts like he hates me the next. I think he has some mental illness and I hope you will be able to support him when I'm gone, if I'm gone. Take good care of him if I don't get to stay and grow old with him. That will be the best thing you could do for me, take care of you and my husband if I don't get to keep him as my husband."

CHAPTER 13

The Decision

A ndrew bought me a pair of sweats and a sweatshirt from the hospital gift shop, in a God awful bright yellow orangish mustard color, but at least they were clean and didn't expose my backside to the rest of the world. They were a little big on me, but he was careful to get them big enough to go over my arm and leg casts.

Andrew had been a butthead in the past, but since he's stopped drinking, he's really a great guy. He's been an invaluable friend to me, even though he's Jacob's best friend and brother.

He was funny and he could make me laugh even when it hurt to laugh, it still felt wonderful to know there was joy out there. Better yet, there were good guys out there that cared about me and treated me with respect.

I didn't want to think about my future, it was too heartbreaking to think past now, but Andrew has been like a medicine for my soul. I don't know how I would have gotten through all this without him.

Today was the day that my husband decided if we were going to make us work, or if he's sending me on my way packing for a final departure. I hope he picks us, picks me, because even though he's hurt me repeatedly, I love him. He meant everything to me, and I'm crushed that I might be thrown away by him again!

I saw Jacob walking down the hall. I grabbed Andrew and said, it's him, this is it, Andrew please help me to my room quickly. And Andrew, pray! He held the arm with a cast, it was heavy, and steadied me as I hobbled down the hall as quickly as possible. Andrew bent down where I could hear him, and he said "I'll be right outside your room if you need me Sis. I'll try that prayer thing for you".

I just squeezed his hand, and whispered "Andrew, that's the most wonderful thing I've ever heard you say". Then I walked into my hospital room and crawled into my bed, so I was ready to talk with Jacob.

He walked into my room and he kissed me like he loved me, like he cared about me, like he wanted me. I was so happy to be in his arms, feeling his kisses, heat, touch, I wanted him, but he pushed me away, gently and said "Babe, we need to talk". I asked him to help me to get comfortable and situated in bed, because I was physically worn out from walking. My hopes were high, Jacob seemed like he was picking us.

He said, "I see you have my brother as my stand in, posted outside your room."

I knew Andrew could hear us and it made me mad that he would say such hurtful words about his own brother. "Jacob, before you start chewing up and spitting out your whole family, why don't we just focus on us for right now and your decision, can you do that?"

"There isn't a lot to say. I love you; you should know that by now. You love the drama sort of like a moth to a flame, and I work almost constantly to get you out of messes. But I love you anyway."

"This is what took you a day to think about and tell me. Why would you say such hurtful things to me, your wife? Let me get this right, you are saying that I'm a drama queen and a klutz and yet you can find it in your heart to love me despite my personality. How kind and generous of you Jacob, I really appreciate your sacrifice on my behalf."

"Well, you are Ms. I want the truth, whole truth, and nothing but the truth, but you can't handle the truth!"

"Okay Jacob, that's fair and I'm sorry. I interrupted you, please tell me what you want to say, I'm listening, and I'll try not to interrupt."

"You want to control me, control us by demanding I go get "help." I don't need help. You love me, I love you, we are married. Married couples go through rough patches. I will see a marriage counselor with you, but I'm not seeing a shrink for me. That's a fair compromise. What do you say to that? Are you willing to go to a counselor for me? A compromise we can both live with?"

"If you think I want to control you, you are just proving once again that you don't know me at all, Jacob, you are wrong. And you are wrong about thinking that you don't need mental help. I do love you, that's not in question here, but you are becoming mean spirited and you don't see things concerning me the way I see things.

I was clear about my condition to stay with you. You once again, kicked me out of your life, now for the second time. But you are telling me a big fat "no" to my heartfelt plea for us to be together."

"I will miss you, and miss the love we have shared, but I've been in this situation before, and the only one who gets hurt in the end is the one who is living in this reality and giving away her youth, energy, time, efforts and love for someone who doesn't appreciate or understand her sacrifices for him.

Jacob, you've given me no choice, I need a divorce. I'm the one broken and in the hospital and you walk away just fine, this pattern can't continue. If you won't go get help, I have to help myself. You took away the choice I had to stay with you. You need to leave, goodbye Jacob!"

"You are kidding! Jenna, tell me this is just that time of the month and it's your drama. You can't be serious."

"There is nothing funny about this, no I'm not kidding. I keep pouring out my heart to you and all you hear is that I'm the problem, I'm trying to control you, that I'm needy and in messes and that I like the drama.

You twist everything I say, and I want to leave before you twist our past into something I will regret. Jacob we have that, don't take that away from us. You were the love of my life, and I honestly don't know how I will get over you."

"I don't know what to say."

"Jacob you won't get help so please just leave. I don't want to cry in front of you and I don't want you to think I'm trying to manipulate you. Please just leave."

He got up, just looked at me with a questioning look on his face and walked out of the room. I heard him tell Andrew in the hall, "You're up Andrew, she ready for second string." Then Jacob stuck his head back into my room and said, "By the way Jenna, Happy Anniversary Sweetheart!" And he turned around and walked out of my room and out of my life.

Andrew walked into my room, but I was hugging a pillow, my face pushed deep in the pillow so I wouldn't scream for Jacob to come back to me. I had a pillow in my face so I didn't yell and cry like a crazy woman who just lost everything important to her. Andrew kindly just slipped out of the room like a gentleman, not a word, just out of sight so I could pull myself together.

I'm getting a divorce, again. I've failed at marriage twice. I failed, I'm a failure at the one thing that really matters. Why is it that I can't find a man to love me? I was just getting my heart rate calmed down so the machine wouldn't make that terrible beeping sound and my phone rang. I looked it was my attorney. I answered, "Mr. Strausz, the divorce is on. I'll be leaving as soon as I'm dismissed from the hospital and have my car fixed."

"I'll send the papers to Jacob and will call you when I hear from Jacob's lawyers."

"Thank you again for helping me."

My phone was buzzing, I looked at call waiting, and it was Brandon.

"Mr. Strausz, I have another call. Do you need anything else?"

"No, I'll be in touch."

"Hello."

"Jenna its Brandon, how are you doing?"

"Actually, I just got off the phone with my divorce attorney, and he's sending papers to Jacob as we speak. I'm just trying to stay calm and not fall apart. How's your day Brandon?"

"I hope you don't mind Jenna, but I'm here."

"What do you mean here?"

"I knew today would be extra tough on you since it's your anniversary, so I wanted to be here for you." I looked toward my doorway and there he was walking into my room. He had phone in hand, smile on his face, and walked to the foot of my bed."

I hung up the phone. Brandon came over to the right side of my bed that didn't have casts and gave me a big hug. I just held on to him like he was the air I needed to breathe. I couldn't let him go. He was nothing but good and kind to me, loving and patient, and I threw him away for Jacob. I hurt him and his daughter, but he's never once thrown that back in my face and he's here for me.

Now when I need him, he's here for me. He is a good man, no he's a wonderful man. When I thought I could talk without crying, I loosened my death grip on him and said "Brandon, thank you for not hating me. I left you, and here you are for me, you are such a good man, a great friend and I don't deserve you."

"Jenna, is that what we are, just friends?"

"Brandon I'm legally married, getting a divorce, and no, you are more than a friend. You know that, but please don't make me give you more than what I can right now. I married someone I thought I knew most of my life, and he has thrown me away twice. Please don't make me talk about you and me right now, I just don't think I can go there.

I need time. I'm sorry if this hurts you, but I have to be honest with you and myself. You are wonderful, and I am broken. Look at me. You know I have to deal in honesty and that's all I've got Brandon. I'm physically and emotionally broken. I hate for you to see me this way, but I'm glad you're here."

"Jenna, I'm here to help you not to increase your stress levels. You called me that's why I'm here for you and only you. What do you want or need me to do? Just tell me and I'll do it."

"I need help getting back home, and by home, I mean Missouri. My car was totaled in the wreck, but Jacob said the insurance company was sending a check for replacement value." Andrew walked in the room and I re-introduced the boys from the New York Art exhibit.

"Andrew, I need my car to get home. Jacob said he had a check from the insurance company. Would you call him and see if you could get that check so I can pay for my replacement car and get out of his life as soon as possible. Can you do that for me Andrew, or should I just call my attorney? I don't want to come between you and Jacob. I just need to move on, he won't get professional help, I have no choice, and I have to go."

"I'll make a call and see what I can do. If there's a problem, then you can call your attorney."

"Thank you, Andrew! You've been a God send, I love

and appreciate you more than you'll ever know!"

Andrew looked at Brandon, and asked "Are you staying here with Jenna, while I'm gone? I think I'll have better luck talking to him in person, so I need to find him."

"Yes, I'll be here."

"Okay, I'll see you both later."

Andrew left for Jacob's house, to get my stuff and my check to get a car and Brandon took my hand.

"Jenna, are you in danger here?"

"I don't think so, what made you ask that?"

"Andrew wanted to make sure you had someone with you while he was gone. Has he been here the whole time you've been in here?

I stopped and thought, "Yes, he has. If he wasn't here, his brother Eddie has been with me every day. Brandon, do you think Jacob's brothers think Jacob could hurt me?"

"I don't want to alarm you but yes, I do. I'm not trying to scare you, but as soon as Andrew gets back, I'm having a private conversation with him. You are fine, I'm here and you are going to be okay, I promise you Jenna."

I pushed the nurse button. "

Nurse Michelle, do you know when my doctor is doing his rounds. I need my dismissal papers. I have a pressing matter that needs my attention, and I need to leave right away. Is there anything you can please do to expedite my dismissal paperwork?"

"I'll check for you Mrs. Jamison."

I wanted to throw up when she called me that. Could Jacob hurt me? How crazy is he? Why would his brothers give me round the clock protection unless maybe he's given them a reason to think he could do something stupid?

Am I making this way bigger than it is? I've got to calm down and trust God to take care of me, because I seriously don't think I can deal with one more real or imagined thing. Not one more thing, I'm a literal wreck!

"I don't know if this helps you or not, but I love you. I

have loved you since our first dinner together and I still do. I know you love me, and the Jacob you first met, but he's changed and you are stronger than you know. I am not putting pressure on you, but I'm not going to allow him, to hurt you anymore.

You tried to make it work with him. Now let your attorney deal with him and his attorney. I will help you with whatever you need, money, anything, just tell me what you want and need. I'm here for you and always will be."

"Brandon, thank you for coming and being here for me, would you think I'm horrible if I asked you to crawl up in this bed and just hold me? I just feel so empty, I ..."

Brandon was already in bed next to me, and he said the most perfect thing he could have ever say to me. "Jenna, I know who you are. You don't have to worry about me not knowing you or thinking you are someone or something you're not. I know you, then he touched my heart gently with his finger tips and he said I know the woman who is loving and generous, smart and beautiful. Jenna, I know you."

I just melted into his arms." I don't know how long we were there, but I was asleep in his arms when Andrew came back into the room. Andrew stood up and motioned for Brandon to come out of the room. I didn't want to know what they were saying.

I didn't want to know if I was in physical danger. I already have a broken heart and broken bones, I don't have far to be broken completely forever. I have two intelligent men here helping me, they can deal with the darkness for me for an hour or so, I need to sleep, and I feel so exhausted. When I woke Andrew was just leaving.

"Hey Andrew, how did it go?"

"Everything is taken care of. Jacob gave me your insurance check and a personal check to get you back on your feet while you try to get your old job back and to pay bills. He's going to be okay Jenna, and you will be fine too.

But you should go back to Missouri and start over. I will miss you."

I sat up and hugged him. "Thank you, Andrew, for everything, and please see if you or your family can get Jacob the help he needs."

Jenna, we've tried for years before you, to get him help, but when you came along, we thought our prayers had been answered. We should have told you about him, but you were happy and so was he, for a while, he really was happy, and Jenna that was all you. Jenna you will always be my sister."

I was crying again, but silent tears this time. I whispered "you will be my family too Andrew. Give me a while to heal, and then I want you to keep in touch. I do love you and Eddie. You both are special to me too."

Andrew leaned down close and whispered in my ear, "Jenna, I've talked with Brandon, watched how he is with his daughter, and with you, and he's a good man. I can relax knowing you can be happy again. You will trust yourself again. I know the road to recovery and it's a daily choice and it's hard every day, but every day it gets a little bit easier. Jenna, you are going to be fine."

"Thank you, Andrew, I am so glad you are healthy, I love who you are now, and you are a man any woman would be lucky to love. Don't let anyone or anything tear you away from your steps to a healthy happy you. You deserve the best."

He just squeezed me tight and said, "love you too". Then he walked out of my room and out of my life.

The doctor walked into the room and said, "I heard you are ready to go home. Is this your husband? I just shook my head no, and he said, "Oh sorry". "I have signed your release papers and you are free to go."

"Thank you, doctor, I will be driving home to Missouri today".

"Jenna, if that is true, you need to make sure you get out

every hour and walk so you don't develop blood clots. After your injuries, a long drive like that could cause you to form blood clots, leading to a stroke even death. I can't let you go if you don't assure me that you will follow doctor's orders."

"Are you serious? Every hour, isn't that a little extreme?"

"I'm not kidding you. And be sure to keep hydrated, drink plenty of water and get out and walk every hour to keep your blood circulating. That is my professional advice to my patient who was nearly killed in a car wreck less than a week ago. Your body is fragile right now Jenna, you need to take it easy for a while. You are a smart woman you need to follow my care plan for your healthy recovery."

"Okay doctor Mike, thanks for the information."

"I'll put in an order for a wheelchair to wheel you down to the front entrance. At that time, you are free to walk out of here forever." He walked out and I stood up.

"Brandon, did Andrew give you the check for my car, because I have no way to get home without it?"

"Yes, I have the check. I called the local dealership, and they don't have the same car with the exact options you had, but they have one that has a few more options that they said they'd throw in for you due to your accident and hospital stay.

Andrew and Eddie both called and talked to the owner personally, and I think he was a friend of the family. They may have paid him some money on their own, I don't know, but those guys are good guys, and they love you, Jenna."

We took a taxi from the hospital to the local dealership, and I gave Pedro my check. He was an older man and he just kept hugging me and saying he was so sorry. I thanked him and asked Brandon to drive my new midnight blue SUV. The tank was full of gas, and we headed out of Kentucky.

I had the clothes on my back and a few things I guess Andrew got from Jacob's, but I didn't want anything that reminded me of my past, not anymore. I was done with Jacob, and the past. I was literally moving on, going forward and I'm not looking back, decisions were made, mistakes, deceptions, truths and friendships. It's over and now with zero miles on my car, I am starting over now.

Brandon wouldn't leave the lot until I was in my seat and in my seatbelt. Being in the car reminded me of my other car, and how my dogs died, I missed them, I hope they passed quickly and not a painful loss of life, I can't think about them anymore, it's just too painful. I'm going back to start living again.

Chapter 14

The Old Becomes New

Brandon was driving down the highway and the GPS was up and running great. I'm so glad he is computer smart so he could figure out all the new features on my fancy car. He knew how to work all the gadgets on my new Midnight Blue SUV. I couldn't keep a thought in my head. I didn't want to just ramble and ramble, so I just sat there in silence.

"Do you want to listen to some music?"

"Sure," I knew he had to be bored out of his mind. He turned on the tunes and they really helped lift my spirits. music transcends me to a higher place. I could almost pretend it was a normal day and I was on a road trip. I loved my new car and that new car smell. My new car looked a lot like my old one, but it was a year newer, had the same two-toned tan leather seats that are heated and cool with the flip of a switch. It's new and paid for so I don't have to worry about a dependable car or car payments.

I'm glad it's not the car Jacob and I picked out together, this is a new car for my new start and it's midnight blue on the outside so no more Red. "Red" is dead and so is my past.

Brandon had made sure we stopped every hour for me to walk around the car, or go to the bathroom, so our trip was taking longer than normal. We had driven a couple of hours and I told him I was starving and needed a Diet Dr. Pepper.

"I'm getting hungry too, what sounds good to you?"

"Spaghetti and meatballs, garlic cheese bread, salad, sound good to you? "

"Yes! Any idea where we are going to find that?"

"Next town I say we get off the highway and explore, do you have time to do that?"

"I have all the time you need. That is not an issue!" The next big city we see a sign for Olive Garden, and we drove directly to that destination, love my GPS. By the time we got there, shock of all shocks I changed my mind and ordered eggplant parmesan and it was delicious.

Brandon had lasagna and spaghetti and I had a bite of his. It was all hot and flavorful. Then we shared a piece of tiramisu that was moist and delicious. Good food, comforting and filling. I hadn't eaten breakfast because I was waiting for Jacob's decision. Then lunch came and I was so upset I couldn't eat, so this early dinner hit the spot for me.

"Thank you for being here with me, I don't know what I would have done without you. What's Kourtney know and think about all of this?"

"She loves you. She knows what Jacob did to you at the Art exhibit and she said "that just isn't right dad!" Then when you called me and told me he kicked you out in the rain, upset and then a car wreck, and that you were in the hospital, she said "dad, what are you doing here, go and get her!"

I couldn't take it anymore. I grabbed my cloth napkin at

the table and covered my face so I wouldn't cry and embarrass Brandon. He didn't care what anyone thought; he quickly walked around the table and hugged me. "Baby I'm so sorry, I shouldn't have told you what she said. You've had an emotional bunch of days. I'm sorry."

"No, I love your daughter and she is so sweet and smart, I just hate that I...I've caused you both pain I'm the one who is so sorry."

"Stop, we don't need to go there, are you finished eating? We should get back on the road."

"Okay, you're right." I wiped my tears, we got up and used the restroom and left for more miles down the highway.

We drove for another five hours or so and I asked if we could stop and get a room? We could get double beds, single bed, king bed, I didn't care I was just so tired. I had no tooth brush, clean under wear, pajamas, nothing. Brandon recommended that we stop at Target and pick up a few things, so I was comfortable tonight.

"Thanks, I'd appreciate that." I leaned on a cart and we walked through the clothes aisles and got undies, bras, toothbrush, deodorant, socks, a couple of pair of jeans and a couple of cute shirts. We grabbed a bag of chips and Diet Dr. Peppers.

Brandon still liked water but now was a Diet Dr. Pepper fan too. We stocked up on some chocolate bars and bottled waters and headed to the check outs then out to my beautiful new car.

We got out to the car, and I asked, "where is Molly and Moose?" For a moment I'd forgotten they were dead. Brandon just stared at me, not saying a word. I realized my mistake and just got back into the front seat shaking my head. He got into the car and said, you have to be exhausted, we need to find a hotel and get some rest. Brandon wanted to stay in a nice place, so he pulled into a Hilton.

I didn't care I just wanted clean and comfortable. I just wanted a shower but how with a cast on my leg and arm? Brandon called room service and got trash bags for my casts. You would think with all my experience with my broken ankles that I would be better at this, but it's such a hassle.

I wanted help getting naked so I could get in the shower, but Brandon said there was no way he could see me naked and be a gentleman, so I took forever but managed a shower. I dressed in my night shirt and made it possible for Brandon to get his shower. He got in the shower and when he got out I was already in bed fast asleep.

I woke up many hours later with an excruciating painful leg cramp, it had only happened to me once before, so I knew what it was. I jumped out of bed, unsure of my surroundings in a hotel room trying to find a light.

Brandon jumped up, "what's wrong?"

"Cramp, I have a bad leg cramp."

Which leg?"

"The one with no cast." He ran over and massaged my leg, I had instant relief. "Thank you, that feels much better. He sat up and looked at me. I'm sure I looked a mess, but he took his finger and traced my lips, and I could feel a part of me come to life.

He sweetly moved my hair behind my ear and started kissing my neck, he was always an excellent kisser. We were kissing and hugging and squeezing when I got another leg cramp and jumped up.

"I need a banana from room service for potassium."

He got on the phone and called, "anything else?"

He ordered oatmeal and a banana and orange juice as soon as possible. And hung up the phone and rubbed my leg. "Any better Babe?"

"Much" with a big smile and he just shook his head. "What time is it?"

"Almost 4:00 a.m. Sorry to have woken you from your sound sleep. You are driving and you need your sleep so try to go back to sleep and I'll eat some food and be fine."

"Are you kidding me? You've started my launch sequence you really want me to go to sleep?"

"Not really, I just wanted to give you that option."

"Get over here," and with that we were reunited, and I didn't care that I was still married. I didn't care that I was exhausted, I was just selfish and wanted a man to want me, to know me and love me.

I didn't want to use Brandon, I cared about him, and he loved me. We had a very wonderful familiar reunion. I don't know how he worked around my casts and leg cramping but my pleasure was intense and his kisses were unforgettable. There was a quiet knock on the door.

Brandon grabbed a towel and gave the man a tip and carried the food into the room. He had crisp bacon on the plate too. We shared the food, I ate the full banana. And after some more massaging of my leg and other areas we re-established our full body contact activities and we were one again. We curled up in one another's arms and slept till after 9:00. We woke up but this time he "helped" me in the shower. It was much easier with two.

I'm still officially married. This is my new beginning and if it hadn't been for Jacob, Brandon and I would have been together a year and a half earlier. I should have never left Brandon, how can he ever forgive me? How can he trust me after what I did to him? To his daughter. "Brandon?"

"Yeah babe."

"I'm so sorry for hurting you and breaking our trusting relationship. I promise you I will never do that to you ever again."

"I know. That's the past we are starting a new. It is sort of like the first time because it's been so long, but you have to know that I love you darling."

"I love you too, I just don't want you to feel like you are my rebound. You are here for me and I appreciate it. And I do love you and always have that was never our problem."

"I know, we need to get dried off and have a brunch and hit the road because we have a long drive ahead since we need to stop and let you get out and walk around every hour for your healing process. No blood clots Jenna, you need long term healthy, and I'm here to make sure that happens."

"Okay, but I just need three more full on kisses and I can get ready and go." After three intense luscious kisses we were out of control and all over each other again. It was rapture! We finally just threw on clothes and walked out of the room so we could just get on the road. We ate in the hotel café and headed down the road.

As we traveled down the road I asked Brandon what he wanted when it came to me and him and our future. I needed him to be honest and clear with any short term or long term plans, if he had any ideas for our future if he saw a future with me at all.

He said, "I've given that a lot of thought and told myself if I ever had a chance to be with you again, I would love you like we were the only two people in the world and never let you go. I made mistakes Jenna, but I only thought I was doing what was best for you at the time. I love you and want you with me, today, tomorrow, next week and forever. This is not a proposal; because you are still officially married to him, but I will get it right this time.

I know what it's like to have you in my life and what it's like to live without you, and I don't ever want to live through the loss of you ever again. You stole my heart and part of my soul and my daughter loves you too. I'm here for you. You don't have to rush into our relationship, because I'm secure, and healthy and not afraid of our future.

We have time to date for as long as you want or need. We have every day of forever. Jenna, this is an offer open anytime, but if you want to move in with me, and live together I would love that, but if you want to be single and on your own again for a while, I can respect that too. I want you to be happy and healthy. I will be here for you for whatever you want and need. I know you and love you."

"You called me when you were excited about your Art exhibit. You wanted to share your life with me, and I was beyond myself making sure that I could get to New York to show you that I still loved you and I was still here for you. Do you know what you want? What do you see for your near and future?"

"I see a Diet Dr. Pepper in my near future, and a bathroom. I don't mean to make light of our conversation, but I need to be comfortable and I really need to use the restroom too. I'll get comfortable, and then we can continue this conversation that I very much want to have with you!"

After we were both back in my car, I felt more relaxed and rehydrated with my caffeine fix. We were able to continue our conversation about our future. "I do love you and that hasn't changed. We have chemistry, and we always had good communication. I love how smart and caring you are with your daughter and me.

I have made mistakes that almost cost me my life, and I'm sorry my poor choices have hurt you and Kourtney. We have a bond that is rare in this life. I want to be with you and your daughter, I adore her, she is precious, and I would never intentionally hurt her. I want you to know you can count on me, I'm not going back, ever."

"However, I'm still married, and I thought I knew Jacob, and come to find out he's certifiably mentally ill. You know what I just remembered, I asked him when we first started dating what was wrong with him, why a rich good looking man had never married and if he had mental illness in his family and he lied to me. No wait he didn't lie to me, he just didn't answer my question. He just laughed out loud, it was a lie of omission, purposefully mislead me, that's a lie in my book."

"Whatever we are, we must be honest every step of the way, every day with each other. I've been married twice now, and I have two failed marriages. It takes two to make a marriage work, and I have two strikes against me. I can't get married again anytime soon. I need time to examine what I keep doing wrong, so I don't do it again.

The most important decision a person can make, and I've failed at it twice. I don't want to fail with you, and I'm starting out with a strike against me for leaving the way I did. You have a child and I don't want to do anything that would adversely affect you or her in a negative way ever again. I refuse to hurt you like that ever again."

"I think I should go back to my house and see if I can make it feel like home again. Although I don't want to buy a bunch a furniture when I just have to get rid of it all when we move in together, so I don't know for sure what I want. I'm still working out all the details in my head. Talking out loud helps me process.

I don't know how I'll feel about waiting to officially start our life together either. I know my dogs being gone will be a big void when I get home. I need time to grieve the loss of my marriage, my dogs and get my heart ready to live and love again. I don't want to short change you in any way Brandon. I see myself with you I just need us to take it slow when it comes to wedding stuff. I don't want to be without you, I just can't say "I Do" anytime soon. I need to heal.

Please don't be hurt with that, it's not that I don't want to live happily ever after with you, but I need my head and heart back to do that. I know you've been more than patient with me, I'm just asking for a little longer. I know you are wonderful and I'm the one who made the wrong choice that put us in this situation.

I know that my decisions have brought us here and I'm

so sorry for my past mistakes. I don't want to make mistakes when it comes to our future together. What are you thinking now that I have talked non-stop for the last hour?"

"I hear what you're saying, and I agree with you totally. If you want to do sleep overs or stay at my house until you feel ready to stay at your house alone, I'm flexible to do whatever you want and need. I've told you that and I mean it. If I thought you were playing games or using me, I would be out, but I know you, your heart, and I love you.

We can work out our future together, day by day. It doesn't have to be in stone this very minute, for now we can take it day by day. We are committed to one another and after your official divorce comes through, we can revisit this conversation anytime you feel ready for that next step."

"That sounds perfect. I love and adore you, and in case I didn't tell you this earlier, thank you for being here for me and thank you for loving me. As much as I'm hurting now, I know I will be able to trust myself to love again, fully unreservedly, and I want to be able to give you all of me.

But first things first, I need a divorce and time to forgive myself for my past. Right now I don't feel like I deserve you or deserved to be loved, so I need to heal. That's as honest and open as I know how to be. I trust you completely or I wouldn't expose my open wounds to you without being guarded and cautious.

I don't worry about that with you. I know you love me and that you are here for me. I gain untold strength by being with you. I don't think you have any idea how wonderful you are Brandon. And I look forward to our future to show you just how much you really mean to me. Just give me time, your love and time that's what I need."

"I've told you there is no pressure from me. We are together in my mind and heart and a piece of paper won't change how I feel for you. You have been lied to and I want you healthy and healed and whole to start your life with me and Kourtney. A new beginning.

There is one more thing we need to discuss before we move on. I've been dating Kayla while you were off living in another state and married to another man. I care about her, she's wonderful, but I love you. She knows I left town to come get you and I haven't talked to her since we've been together, but I wanted you to know I care about her too."

"I wouldn't expect you to stop your life just because I ran off and got married. I'm glad you found comfort and happiness, and I liked Kayla too except, not as much now, but she is a beautiful and nice woman. I sort of feel jealous, but I know I don't have the right to feel that way. I'm just going to smile and thank you for your full disclosure. Hmm, so are we dating, engaged, exclusive, what are we Brandon?"

"I wondered how long it would take you to bring that up after you found out about Kayla," and Brandon laughed out loud. We can be whatever you want."

"Clearly, I want you and I don't want to share, but I've already asked too much of you as a friend and a lover, I'll let that be your decision. It's all up to you and what you need and want, I don't want to be selfish."

"I don't see where we need to make that decision at this exact moment so we can wait on that call."

"That's fine but what I hear you saying to me is that you don't want to end it with Kayla. That's fine we aren't exclusive but just be honest, tell me the truth not what you think I want to hear. No games between us. I know you are sexy and could kiss a saint into a sinner, so I understand your manly needs and desires. I only wanted to be the one who you wanted but I deserve what I get."

"Kayla isn't a punishment to you marrying Jacob. She was a friend who knew you and could help me get through my sorrow when you left me without any warning. She was sweet and affectionate, and…"

"Brandon don't tell me anything else about you and another woman, not right now. Let's just listen to some music for a while."

"I'm sorry. What kind of music so you want to listen to?"

"Country, no let's find a classical station if that's alright with you. Pure music with no words, just instruments would be great right now."

We drove for about an hour and no talking just music and looking out the windows. It was getting dark outside and I was tired and we were going to need to stay on the road one more night because when you stop every hour it takes more time than expected to get out, walk around, stand in line to use the restrooms and get more food to munch on in the car.

"Can we stop for the night and get a good nights' sleep; we should make it home tomorrow if you are okay with that?"

"Sure."

We pulled over at a Holiday Inn Plus and had a nice clean room and two queen beds in a room. I got in the shower and cried for an hour, got out and put my pajamas on and got into bed. When I came out of the shower, Brandon had a banana and a box of cereal, a bowl and a container of milk for me by my bed. I just laughed out loud, "that was so thoughtful, thank you."

"If you're through in the bathroom I'll jump in."

Go ahead, and thanks Brandon, I appreciate you driving all day, I know that can be tiring."

"I'm fine Jenna, you eat your banana and crash if you're tired."

"Okay, good-night, sweet dreams."

"Good night, dream sweetly."

CHAPTER 15

DIVORCE

I woke up in a hotel room with a man I loved, but that wasn't my husband. He has a girlfriend and doesn't want to be exclusive. I'm married but I'm getting a divorce again. Wow that sounds like it should be words to a country music song, but no one would believe it.

I don't know how it's possible, but honestly my heart has changed for my soon to be ex-husband. I don't feel the same for Jacob since my car wreck. Something inside of me died and the special place in my inner most heart and soul that only Jacob held, is broken forever. That heart connection, trust, and honesty the love is gone and I'm running on empty.

Jacob became a man who didn't make rational conversations and didn't love me or want me. Maybe I make good men go bad I don't know. He wouldn't get professional help and our conversations were not loving and kind like when we were first married.

Two years of being in love with him, the ups and downs,

the ins and outs of our relationship and it's finally over. I should be devastated. I should be destroyed. My body and heart have been through the wringer, but since I've left Kentucky, I feel like I really am breathing deeper, and feeling happy and hopeful.

How is that even possible with everything I've been through? I'm not fearful about my future, I feel like I was on a detour, a Jacob detour, and now I'm back on track. I'm headed in the right direction for me and I'm happy. I don't know how, but my heart must be stronger than I thought it could be. It's a merciful God thing for sure.

I got up went to the bathroom and put on a pair of jeans and a new shirt I bought at Target. I had to buy a bigger size jean to get over my cast, but with a belt around my waist, these jeans are comfortable and look much better than the sweats I had. I never knew they had cute clothes at Target.

I felt pretty and comfortable in this blouse. I do need to contact Jacob to ask him to send me my clothes. I don't have money to buy all new everything, what was I thinking? I know what I was thinking "Get the heck out of Dodge, do not pass go, do not collect $200.00!"

I felt like Brandon had acted distant last night after I'd poured out my heart to him all day long. I hate that I overwhelm men. I'm more "drama" than any one man wants to deal with. When will I learn to keep my mouth shut and not be so open and honest? No man wants to know every thought and feeling I'm having every day.

I don't think I do that all the time, but with Brandon, I did process all of my feelings verbally yesterday. Poor guy was stuck in the car with me and couldn't get away for a break. Just me yack, yack, yack. Maybe he's quiet because I didn't give him a chance to speak much yesterday?

I came out of the hotel bathroom dressed and ready for our last day on the road.

"You look pretty and refreshed. Are you ready for

breakfast?"

"It's so nice to start the day with a compliment, thank you for that! Now let's go eat breakfast, I'm starving." A free complementary breakfast comes with our room, so we went downstairs and had our fill of oatmeal, eggs, bacon and I had a couple pancakes too. I love pancakes. I drank milk, coffee and orange juice. Made sure I made a bathroom break before we got back on the road. We filled up with gas and hit the highway for home.

I had my phone in my purse and it was charged up overnight so when it rang it scared me. I saw it was from my attorney, so I needed to take the call. "Brandon, I need to take this call, it's my attorney."

"Do you want me to pull off the road and I can get out to give you some privacy."

"I have no secrets from you, if you don't mind, I'll just put him on speaker."

"Jenna, this is Sonny, I just got your divorce papers back from your husband and he's agreed to everything and wants to pay spousal support too. You didn't ask for it, but you need it. Take my advice and sign the papers. I need a number to fax you this document so you can sign it and send it back to me as soon as possible."

"Sonny, I can't right now, I'm on the road almost back to Missouri. Why the urgency?"

"You need to find a place with a fax machine maybe a bank, so that I can fax you the papers and you sign them before he changes his mind. You know Jacob, the yo-yo, one minute divorce, the next not, we may only have a narrow window of opportunity here before he changes his mind. I highly recommend you pull over and call me back in the next thirty minutes with a number that I can send you the contract and you can send a signed copy faxed back to me.

I will send official papers to your home address in Missouri and that will be for the filing at the courthouse, but I want to get this transaction completed before a judge friend of mine leaves today and he's in town until 4:00. Call me when you have a number for me to fax the paperwork. You pay me good money, follow my advice, and get to a bank as soon as possible."

"Okay, we will pull off the road as soon as we see the next town, find a bank, and get a fax number for you to send me the paperwork. I'll sign the divorce papers and get them notarized there at the bank and send them back to you immediately. I think we should find a bank in the next 20 minutes. I'll call you as soon as those arrangements are made, thanks".

I hung up the phone and asked Brandon if he heard all the conversation. We needed to find a bank as soon as possible so my attorney can send me the divorce papers from Jacob and his attorney. Sonny thinks Jacob could change his mind about the divorce and withdraw his written offer with him being so unstable, so we need to do this now. Mr. Strausz said time was of the essence."

Brandon was nothing but supportive as usual. "Okay and we were at a bank, inside getting a vice-president to help us with the faxing, notary and refaxing my paperwork to my attorney in Kentucky within an hour".

I called Sonny, to verify he received my signed divorce papers from the fax number he gave me, and he was already in his car on the way to the courthouse to meet the judge. He said I could be officially divorced by the end of the day. I couldn't believe it. I guess small towns run a lot different than bigger cities do.

"Would you please call me and let me know when I'm officially single again, when my divorce is final?"

"Yes, I'd be glad to call you, or my secretary will call, but one way or another, you will know."

I just looked at Brandon and said, "I cannot believe this, but I could be officially divorced in the next hour. I can't believe it's happening so fast. I'm not even home yet and

I'm going to be divorced. It's like I am in a dream that's part dream, part nightmare and I can't wake up. I feel so …" (stop talking Jenna, don't be drama, too much for men).

"Jenna you are shaking, we need to eat some healthy food, not gas station junk food. What do you want?"

"I don't care, you drive I'm with you. I just don't want to make any decisions right now. We stopped at one of my favorite sandwich shops, Panera, and I had chili and mac and cheese, comfort food and delicious. Brandon ate a grilled chicken sandwich, such a healthy conscience. We were almost finished eating and my phone rang, it was Sonny.

"I just called to tell you that you are now officially divorced. I know you are on the road, but I told you I'd call you. You are now officially single and divorced. I'll send you the paper work to your house and my bill. If you need me for anything else, feel free to call me. I wish you the best Jenna."

"Thank you for all your help Sonny, I really appreciate it, good-bye." I hung up the phone and looked at Brandon sort of in shock. "Brandon, it's official, I'm divorced."

"How do you feel about that?"

"It's like Kentucky never really happened. It's over erased and I'm saying goodbye to my past".

"I know what's happening here, I just want to know what you are thinking, and how you are feeling about everything."

I looked down at the table, "Brandon I don't want to overwhelm you. Jacob told me I was always in a mess and I was overwhelming. I noticed you were very quiet last night, and there is nothing wrong with that, it's just I told myself that I needed to back off and not talk so much so I didn't overwhelm you too. I don't want to make the same mistakes with you".

Brandon reached across the table and took both my

hands, and I had to look him in the eyes. "Jenna, you are holding back, not sharing with me because you are afraid that you are too much for me to deal with, is that what you're saying?"

"Yes, I don't know, maybe, probably I am. You chose to be quiet and reserved last night to process everything, and I respected your time and space. I get it. I guess I just wanted to give myself some personal time to process all this without having to voice and label every feeling and thought I was having too".

"Jenna, you are not going to overwhelm me, you forget I have a teenager. You don't need to ever hold back from me. I want to know all of you and if things ever do get to be too much, you won't have to worry, I'll tell you right then and there at that time. I am secure and can speak up and step up whatever is needed.

If I need a minute, I'll tell you I need fifteen-minute break to get perspective and cool down. You don't have to fill every moment with telling me how you feel, but I love to know every detail about you and how you see things. You fascinate me on so many levels, but I do love you for your mind as well as your body, I really do."

I stood up, walked to his side of the table and kissed him gently on his cheek then turned around and I walked up to the counter and ordered a pastry to eat on the road. Brandon continued his eating healthy and didn't want one. I wasn't hungry, I just wanted something sweet. I think stress makes me want sweets.

When I was married to Jacob, I wasn't hungry most of the time, but now I'm divorced, wow. I'm officially divorced, so I guess it's time to take off my beautiful wedding ring. I loved that ring and I loved Jacob more than I loved anyone or anything ever before, and now I can't have either one of those precious jewels. Oh, I'm totally eating this cherry cream cheese danish in the car. "I'll need two bottled waters to go please".

We got back into the car, and drove all the way back to Missouri. Our ride was comfortable but quiet. I slept part of the way, when I woke up, Brandon was on his cell. "I'm sorry if I woke you up."

"No problem, you didn't wake me up."

"Jenna's awake now, so I need to let you go. I'll talk to you soon. Thanks for calling."

I should let him go so he can be with Kayla. She was beautiful, and I liked her before I knew she was dating Brandon. I don't know what he is to me and maybe a new start should be a totally new start without Brandon. I can sell my house and start over anywhere, it's not like I have a job. I need to make my own decisions and know what I want and why I want it.

I need to leave Brandon alone and give him a chance to get away from me and my "drama". No calling him, if he calls me that will be fine, but I'm not going after him. I need to give him a chance to be happy without me. If he wants Kayla, she's a beautiful woman, he can have her. I'm tired not sleepy really, just emotionally and physically tired. I need a mental and emotional break. I don't have the energy to fight for Brandon, no matter how wonderful he is, I just can't.

"I'm guessing you could put two and two together and know that was Kayla on the other end. She wanted me to tell you hello for her, so hello."

"Thanks, and you can tell Kayla thanks for sharing you with me this week so I could get home safe and sound. I appreciate you both and the sacrifices you've made on my behalf."

"Wait, I hear a tone, are you saying you want me to date Kayla? Is that what you are insinuating?"

"No, I'm not telling you what to do, never have, never will. I want you to be happy and only do what you want to do. I'm just saying thank you and she's a great gal, that's all."

"Jenna, she called me, I didn't call her. She hadn't heard from me and wanted to make sure I was okay. I didn't want her to worry and you were asleep, so I answered my phone. I told you before, she's great but she is not you. She's nice and pretty, but she doesn't have your sense of humor, whit or heart. I love you."

"I know you've told me that in the past, but after everything that's happened, I'm thinking Kayla not being me is her best feature right now."

"You have had a very stressful week; a car wreck, lost your dogs, broke your bones and you are now officially divorced. Kayla would never be able to deal with one of those things much less all of them at once and with the kindness that you have handled everyone and everything related to those situations. Jenna, you are a good woman. You are kind, smart most of the time, (winking at me) and you are loved. That sounds like a line from a movie doesn't it? One day you will believe me.

I thought about our earlier conversation, and I want to be exclusive with you. That way you will see that I am serious about you and only you. I'm not Tom, and I'm not Jacob, I'm just me. I'm not perfect, but I will do all I can to provide a loving and stable home for my daughter and for you if you want to be a part of our lives".

"Thank you, Brandon, I know you are a loving, caring wonderful man, and I'd be a lucky woman to be part of your life. If you want to be exclusive just the two of us, I think I could live with that (I said with a big smile)".

"If that's what you wanted, to be exclusive, why didn't you just tell me that in the first place?"

"I told you Brandon, I wanted it to be your choice, your decision! When do we get to start being exclusive now that I'm single?"

"I don't want to rush you or make you feel like I'm putting pressure on you to do what I want. I want you to tell me what you want when you want it, no games. Do you want to stay at my house tonight, or would you rather stay at your house? Do you want to be alone? What do you want? I can't read your mind. I don't even know if you have furniture at your house, or someone living there while you were in Kentucky. Just tell me what you want."

"Honestly, I want to curl up in bed with you. But I've had you all to myself for days on end, and I don't want to be selfish with your time. If you need to go home to be with Kourtney, or say a final farewell to Kayla, I want to be sensitive to your needs and wants."

How about you stay at my place with me tonight and then you and I or just you can go to your house tomorrow and see if you are ready to be back there or not. You are welcome to just move in with me today and start our life together here and now. "It's whatever you want. I really want you in my home, you are already in my heart and soul, just know I want you when you are ready for that step."

"I'd love to stay with you tonight and maybe every other night after that too, but let's just start with tonight. And to make things worse, our first night together in your house may be a night just cuddling together if you are okay with that, I'm just emotionally spent today. Getting a divorce is draining."

"I would love to hold you in my arms all night long, you need to figure out that I love you and I'm happy to be with you. No promises about how cuddly I'll be in the morning, but for tonight you will be safe, you'll be with me."

"Sounds good to me. Are we home yet?"

"I'd say twenty minutes and we should be pulling into my driveway".

We pulled into the driveway, took in the luggage. Then directly to the shower and went straight to bed. We curled up in each other's arms and legs and a few extra pillows to sleep comfortably with casts and slept like only you can when you are in your own bed. I didn't get up until after

12:00 the next day. Brandon had been up and working downstairs in his office. I was shocked I slept so late.

I went to the bathroom, brushed my teeth, combed my hair, and managed another hot shower. Then I got into Brandon's white button-down dress shirt, put on my black Tomboy shorts underwear and unbuttoned the top three buttons and headed downstairs to find my Brandon. The real reason I was going downstairs was to make a cup of coffee! I checked my look in the mirror and even with the casts I looked pretty inviting, hope Brandon feels the same way too.

I went to his office and Brandon was on the phone, but he smiled and held up one finger, his pointer finger, letting me know he'd be with me in a minute. So I headed to the kitchen for coffee. My sweet man had a pot of coffee made and waiting for me and Diet Dr. Pepper stocked in the fridge. I was so excited.

I wanted something hot for the morning or should I say afternoon, so I was on my tip toes reaching for the coffee cups when my man came in the room, slipped up behind me slid his arms down my sides and said in his low and sexy voice, "nice shirt".

I immediately turned around and he lifted me up to sit me down on top of the counter. It was cold on my bare skin and I squealed and that's all it took. He was on me, and we were lost in each other. It felt remarkable to be with this amazing man again. He had skills I didn't remember. I sincerely hope he didn't learn these things from Kayla.

No, stop it Jenna, I'm not going to give Kayla one second of my intimate time with Brandon, not one. When we both had our fill of each other and were laying on the center island countertop now panting for air, I said, "I guess I'll have to wear your shirts more often".

"It's not the shirt, it was you, it's always been you. You were so cute trying to reach the coffee cups; I'll move them to the bottom shelf so you can have your coffee in the morning dear. I want my house to be your house. We can rearrange anything you want. Just let me know and I can help you move things around. I know you are an independent woman, but you have broken bones and don't need to overdo it. Just ask for help when you need it!"

"Brandon, I want to stay here with you, forever, I really do. I don't want to be alone. I don't need to give myself a time out, in isolation at my house. I'm better than okay because of you. I love you and don't want to waste another minute being without you.

I know that this is all crazy and seems too sudden, but Jacob broke my trust of love and honor, and I will never feel the same about him ever again. I will always wish him well and love him in a way, but never trust him with my heart ever again. The Jacob part of my life is broken forever. And I'm shockingly better now than I've been in a long time. How do you feel about all that?"

"I was hoping you would stay with me. I told you I want you and I love you and my house is yours and Kourtneys'. I feel so complete with you here. I'm more than happy I'm fulfilled with you in my heart, life and home. You belong here with me, forever Jenna. We agree that Jacob is your past, and Kourtney and I are your future.

When I tell you that "I do" I really will mean forever, not for two years, not ten years, but forever. You can put your trust in me, I wouldn't lie to you. That's not who I am, you know you can trust me, and be safe and secure in knowing that I love you and no matter what has happened or will happen in our future. I always will love you better or worse, sickness and in health, I love you unconditionally".

"I know and that's why I love you right back. I want to be here with you too, I know that in my heart, mind and soul. I'm not afraid to marry you Brandon, so whenever you want to propose to me, I'm ready to officially start our life together. I'm so sorry for my choices of the past, and all the hurt that has caused, but I'm so glad we are back together at last. I want to move forward with our future together. I love you my handsome sexy Brandon."

The kissing resumed and soon after the coffee was poured, it doesn't get better than afternoon delight!

Chapter 16

The Gift

Brandon, and I got dressed, he offered to go over to my house with me and I told him I'd love for him to come with me, but he'd been with me 24/7 the last 4 days and if he needed a break, I was fine with that. He just laughed and told me we were going to my house first, then grocery shopping to get some food in the house because Kourtney would be at his house this weekend. I couldn't wait to see her.

We pulled up to my house and there were six large UPS boxes sitting on my front porch. I wondered how long they had been sitting there in the weather unattended. Brandon and I just looked at each other and got out of my SUV.

The boxes said one of six, so I knew they were all there. I unlocked the house and Brandon and I dragged the big wardrobe boxes into the house. I opened the first box and it had a letter from Jacob and under the note, was stacks of my clothes, shoes, etc. I sat down on my couch and while Brandon was bringing my other boxes into my house, I read the third and final letter from Jacob.

My Dearest Jenna,

There are so many things I could say, should have said, but we are in the here and now and not the past so here goes. I'm sorry, for things I did and said that were hurtful and mean. Andrew told me what I did and said to you, and I honestly don't even remember doing or saying many of those things to you.

It's like he was telling me about someone I didn't even recognize. I'm glad you are far away from me for your own good. You were and will always be the love of my life and I will always be thankful that I had your love for as long as I did. I'm guessing that you and Brandon will be a couple soon, and as much as I hate him, I know he's a good guy and he will take care of you.

I have money Jenna, and if you ever need anything ever, you let me know and I will send you a check, no questions asked no strings attached. I love you, always have and always will. I'm so sorry Jenna, I should have got the help you asked me to get and you'd be in my life right now. I was a fool and now I know it.

I have had two appointments with a therapist, and she is helping me. I'm also on some medications for something she called bipolar disorder, and I think I feel better and I'm thinking clearer than I have in years. You know I hate medications, but I'm taking them in the hopes that one day, I will be able to be in a long-term healthy relationship with someone that loves me.

I want a chance to love someone without destroying her or nearly killing her like I did to you. Jenna, I'm so sorry for the pain I caused you, please forget all that hurt and pain and only remember the love we shared. We had the best of times. I loved you, still do.

Love you forever,

Jacob

Brandon had brought all the boxes into the house and

was leaning against the kitchen counter watching me as I finished reading Jacob's letter. I just walked over to Brandon, gave him the letter and threw my arms around his waist, put my head against his chest and leaned against him to feel him breath, to feel his strength against me. He put one arm around me and held the letter with the other hand and read my letter. I'm sure he had time to read it more than once, because we stood there for a long time.

My stomach growled and sort of brought us back to alertness. Brandon offered to take me out to lunch. I thanked him for carrying in all those heavy boxes and I was really glad he came with me today, things weren't what I had expected, but when do things really ever go as expected? In my life that rarely happened.

Brandon kissed me and asked, "do you have closure now?"

I let go of him and stepped away from him so I could look him in the eyes. "Brandon, my divorce was closure! Will part of me always care about the man who wrote that letter? Yes, but only the memories.

I have enough love to love you, and your daughter forever. I told you, I don't want you to feel like you are a rebound or a stand in for anyone, and it sounds like you are worried about that being an issue. You must trust me, or we have nothing. I can't be with a man who doesn't trust me. Maybe I should just stay in my house until you feel I've said good-bye to my past, good-bye to Jacob. You just let me know when you can trust me, and we can move forward then".

"You are emotional and hungry, let's eat and finish this conversation after we've had a few minutes to think about what's been said here. I'm not saying you don't have the right to be emotional, you do, it's just I think we will make better decisions if we aren't hungry. I want us to make wise decisions for our future together".

"Fine". (One-word responses from Jenna never a good

sign!)

We went to Applebee's and he ordered a grilled chicken breast, side salad and water with lemon something nice and healthy compared to my meal. I had a cheeseburger and onion rings with a side salad. We were sort of quiet while we ate.

Brandon spoke first. "That was nice of Jacob to write you that note and own up to how things were with you and him honestly. Sorry it took a divorce before he was willing to get help. I'm sure you are thinking, if he would have agreed to get help a week ago, you'd still be married to him now. A lot has happened for you and for us in the last week. I don't want you to feel I'm taking advantage of you during a vulnerable time.

You know how I feel about you. I love you. I want you, all of you and I want you to live with me and love me forever. Are we still on the same page with that or do you feel like you need to step back and give yourself alone time? Maybe go back and give Jacob another chance, now that he is doing what you asked him to do. He got help and is doing better as evidenced by his thoughtful letter to you".

"I can totally understand your confusion with me and my feelings when it concerns Jacob, but I won't be going back to him ever. He threw me away twice and the last time nearly killed me. I don't have a past or a future to go back to with Jacob. You don't have to worry about me going back to a lie; I live in the truth.

I am going forward, and I want you and our life together Brandon. Jacob's letter gave me joy knowing he's getting help and seeing things clearly now that he has medications to help him. But if he stopped taking them or whatever he decides to do, it isn't connected to me anymore.

I'm divorced and that relationship is over, I don't know how to reassure you any other way. My word and my actions are all I have to reassure you that my past is in the past. You are going to have to trust me someday. I know I hurt you deeply once and trust takes time to rebuild, but if we need to slow things down between us and build that trust in our relationship again, I will do what it takes to show you that I'm trustworthy".

"I trust you, with my life, my future, my home, my daughter and my heart. I love and adore you and want you to be happy. I just want us to communicate so we don't have any miscommunications when it comes to you and me and your feelings. How often do men get it right? I feel like I've been given a second chance with you, and I want it. I want us to make beautiful music together, in harmony with our future goals. I love you so much".

"Brandon let's go back to my house. Everything I own is already packed in boxes, so let's just get them and take them to your house and I'll unpack my stuff at your house".

"No, Jenna, let's get your boxes and take them to our home. If you want us to look for a different house, we could sell the one I'm in now and find one you like better".

"No, I already have one house on the market and your home has plenty of room for all of us. It's big enough that we both can have our own space and still be together to make our beautiful music collectively. I love you and your home and our family with Kourtney".

"My house is yours, if you are through eating, let's go get your stuff loaded. We'll call FedEx to deliver your boxes to our house to unpack your stuff and get you settled in before my daughter gets home this weekend. Babe, if you need anything just let me know and we can get it".

"I love you Brandon, I really do, and I want us, and our future. I look forward to growing old with you if you can put up with me that long".

"Third times the charm, we are going to make it. I won't let you go, I won't throw you away. You won't be invisible to me, I will always see you and value you and want you. I know what it is to love you and lose you.

I don't ever want to live without you again. I love you

Jenna, the forever kind of love. My friends say I'm a fool for trusting you after how you left me. But I don't care what they think. After we've been married ten, twenty years we will just prove them all wrong."

"Brandon thank you for believing in me and us. Thank you for standing up for me and always being there for me. I love you more and more every minute we are together. I didn't think that was possible for my heart that's been ripped and shredded recently to come to life much less love so completely."

We got to my house, and we were in my bedroom immediately and into each other like two lovers should be. I experienced the pleasure and freedom to be with a man who is good looking, strong, loving and honest. He has seen me at my very worst, I've broken his heart in the past and he has been there for me anyway, he's amazing. I love him and know I really will have a happily ever after with this man, my Brandon my future. I was a fool, but I will make it up to him.

Before our intimate time together, he called Fed-X to come to my house to transport the six large wardrobe boxes to my new address at Brandon's house. (When the boxes arrived later that day, I unpacked my stuff and I was excited to start our life together.) I got out of my SUV when we got to Brandon's place and Brandon picked me up and carried me over the thresh hold into the house.

Once we were inside the entire house was filled with red heart shaped balloons with long red streamers on each one, I bet there were 500 balloons, it was like walking under a red rainbow. He carried me to the kitchen where we had made love earlier and there was a ring box and lit candles. Brandon put me down then got on one knee and asked me to be his wife, lover, friend and partner in business for the rest of our lives.

He must have had the ring before I left to marry Jacob, because he couldn't have had time to get me a ring since we've been back. He just looked up at me with that smile, all I could say is "yes forever! Forever! I love you Brandon, I do!"

"How did you do all this? I thought this is our house, so I wanted our special moment to start here with just you and me. I hope this meets your dreams."

"You exceed my expectations almost always. It is perfect, I loved the proposal, and the ring, it's beautiful and it fits, see you amaze me. You gave me the best gift you could ever give me, you. I want to spend my life loving you and being your wife. You are so kind, sexy, smart, good communicator, lover, funny, best friend and I'm very blessed, I love you, Brandon."

We kissed and kissed and at that moment I felt complete and at home in my heart. I never would have believed that my heart break from Jacob could dissolve into nothingness in the shadow of Brandon's love. I guess the saying "love conquers all" really is true.

Just then the FedEx driver rang the doorbell, so Brandon said he wanted to bring my boxes upstairs before it started to rain. He just wanted to surprise me with my home proposal and it was perfect for us. Over the top and intimate, that's us in a nut shell. This was a proposal I could tell his daughter, family and our friends too.

When FedEx and Brandon finished carrying in the six refrigerator boxes upstairs to our bedroom, he needed to make room for my clothes in what was once his personal closet. He was so cute, moving his stuff to one side of his large walk-in closet to make room for my side to hang my stuff.

He was very organized, everything in his closet was organized even by color, so I'm sure my closet will be organized like it's never been before, with his side of the closet staring at my side of the closet, and I'm fine with that.

Brandon said I could start unpacking and he'd run to the

store and buy more hangers because clearly we were going to need them for my stuff. Kourtney worked part time at a teen clothing store, and she said she could bring home tons of hangers for free. Brandon told her he would pay for them, but Kourtney's boss said not to worry about it. So he didn't have to go shopping.

Then he told me he had his photography class tonight and needed to get prepared if I could handle the unpacking on my own, he'd head down stairs and get to work on things for class. I asked him if Kayla would be in his class tonight.

He said "yes."

I said "okay," and went back to unpacking.

"Jenna, she's my student, I can't kick her out of my class because I'm in love with you. I would lose my job."

"I know, I didn't ask you to be unrealistic, and I would never ask you to be unprofessional or less than your best ever. I just wanted to know if she would be there, that's all. Will Kourtney be here with us tonight?"

"Yes, do you want me to get someone to cover my class tonight that would be two weeks in a row I've missed my classes, but that way I could be here with you when Kourtney gets home?"

"No, didn't you just hear what I said a minute ago? I'm not so insecure that I can't be by myself. I'm starting to think you don't have confidence in me or who I am when I'm not with a man. I told you that I love your daughter and can't wait to see her. If you are worried about our reunion then stay home with us, but don't paint me to be someone I'm not."

"You are so cute when you get mad. I am sorry fiancé I did hear what you said, I don't think you are insecure without a man, but I just wanted to be supportive and here if you wanted me to be. I know you can handle whatever comes your way. You've proven that in the last couple of weeks to me over and over. I love you my little jealous short-tempered darling".

"Oh, you think I'm short-tempered, do you? I'm not short tempered I'm just passionate about what's right and the truth. I'm passionate about those I love. I'm passionate about you. How much time do you need to get ready for your class tonight?"

With that, Brandon grabbed me and carried me up the stairs to our bedroom. We were laughing so hard I don't know how he didn't drop me. I weigh a ton with my casts on, but he managed me like I was a feather. I love that he is fit and strong. We were quickly in our bed enjoying our impending marriage. We had a wonderful afternoon together.

Then he looked at the clock and said "Jenna, I'm going to be late for my class." I just laughed as he jumped up, threw on his jeans and a shirt slipped on a pair of shoes and ran to his office. He grabbed his bag shook his finger at me and said, "I'll see you tonight my beautiful fiancé."

I hollered down the stairs, "I love you my handsome fiancé."

Kourtney would be here in an hour, I quickly took a shower and threw on a cute outfit to make my first impression as her future stepmom, a good one. Kourtney opened the door and yelled "Dad, Jenna you home?"

I hollered down the stairs, "I'm up stairs" and I heard her running up the stairs, she is so energetic and young! I just came out to the hallway, and she was there hugging me and telling me congratulations on our engagement.

"Jenna, your casts, are you okay?"

"I'll be fine and I'm so glad be home. Kourtney, I love you and your dad. I'm so glad to be part of your family. Thank you for loving me and forgiving me for my past mistakes. I'm sorry I caused you and your dad pain. But you can count on me, I'm here for keeps. I love you both."

"Oh, I know that, we love you too. I helped dad with the proposal balloons and the house is still full of them. Did you like them?"

"Yes darling, I loved the romantic effect. We have tall ceilings so I guess we have to wait until all the helium comes out of them for them to get low enough for us to get rid of them all. But I love the romantic feel it gives our home."

Kourtney looked so cute, her hair pulled back in a ponytail. She was talking non-stop and we walked down to the kitchen to get some food. Kourtney wanted tacos so we started cooking the ground turkey. Brandon eats healthy, I'm going to learn to appreciate healthy eating or die trying. But seriously, I really couldn't tell that big of a difference in our tacos from ground beef to ground turkey meat.

Kourtney and I sat and ate and talked and talked like we were best friends forever. She said she was so glad I was going to be her mom and felt close to me already. She thought I was beautiful and that her dad was never happier than when he was with me. She didn't have to tell me that, but she sort of tells everything she knows.

She feels grown up and that she's got a handle on life and all it has to offer. She has an answer for everything. I remember that self confidence that strength of youth, and all the stupid things I did and said during that time of strong confidence. I took risks I would never take now, oh youth and its wonderful memories.

We were talking about her day and laughing when Brandon walked in the door. He walked in and Kourtney ran to him and gave him a big hug and kiss. I wanted to do that too, but I'm the grown up, so I needed to let her feel like she is the only woman in her daddy's eyes.

Brandon just winked at me and said, "Hi Babe," and walked over to me and kissed me passionately in front of his daughter. I thought this really is going to work. We are going to be a happy family. I love them.

"We fixed tacos together. Kourtney is a great cook. Are you hungry?" So we went back to the kitchen and fixed more tacos for Brandon. We listened to Kourtney talk and catch us up on what was happening in her life. She is very animated, talks with her hands and is really funny. I laughed until my sides hurt. At one point I was crying, and Brandon just put his arm around me and whispered in my ear, "I love you babe." I was at home in his home, in our home.

Kourtney got a text from a boy named Randy and then she said she needed to take the call and left the room for privacy. So we had a few kisses and I let him finish his late dinner before I asked about his evening, his class, and Ms. Kayla. "So how did your class go tonight dear?"

"You mean was Kayla in class, and did I tell her we are engaged?"

"Yes dear, that is exactly what I meant, see how perfectly we communicate?" I just smacked him on his butt.

"I knew exactly what you were thinking when you started biting on your bottom lip. I don't know if you know you do that, but it's sexy as all get out."

I just looked at him. I couldn't tell him that Jacob said the same thing to me, because if it's sexy to him, I want him to enjoy it, I want to enjoy it with him. I just smiled and said, "I didn't realize that I was doing that." It was sort of true, I didn't know I had just done that, so that's the truth I'll hold on to. "Well, was she there, was Kayla in class? Did you tell her? Don't make me beg you."

"You can beg me later tonight when we are in the bedroom."

"Very funny, and don't change the subject, Mr. Professor."

"Yes, Kayla was in class. She came up after class and asked how you were doing? I told her you were great and as of this evening we were officially engaged. She said that happened really quickly and that if things don't work out with you, that I should remember what a great time that she and I had together.

I thanked her and told her I wished her the best and I hoped that she would find someone that would love and respect her always. She did hug and kiss me goodbye and then I walked out to my car to come straight home to you and Kourtney. I love you Jenna."

"Good, because I love you too! I'm not thrilled with another woman kissing you and hugging on you, but since she is your past and I'm your future, I will let that slide this one time. No more kissing from Kayla or any other woman but me, and your daughter, two entirely different kinds of kisses but that should meet all your kissing needs!"

"Yes, Jenna, you and Kourtney are all I need, you got that right babe. With all this talk about kissing, I think you should let me sample your luscious lips immediately."

"You do, do you? After you brush your teeth and get all the Kayla out of your mouth, then I'm all in."

"Oh Jenna!"

Chapter 17

Happily Ever After

Kourtney came into the room and asked if her girlfriends Missy and Beverly could spend the night. Brandon asked her what they were going to do. Just watch movies and talk. He said sure just find out when they are getting picked up on Saturday morning, because we have plans Saturday.

"What are we doing?"

"We are spending family time together, and what better way to bond with two women than to go shopping at the mall and walk around all day and let my two girls' shop."

Kourtney screamed in a high range and very loud happy scream. I didn't know humans could respond in such a fashion. She'd acted like she had just won the lottery and I just laughed.

"I'll do whatever you guys want to do, but honestly I'm not a big shopper. Kourtney might prefer to have her girlfriends shop with her and I could hang back with you, and just sit and watch her go in and out of all the stores in the mall. I've been a teenage girl, this could be an all-day deal, exhausting experience for the "Cast woman". Not really fun getting clothes on and off over an arm and leg cast, sorry I don't want to be a party pooper, just want this to be a fun time for Kourtney."

"Can they go with us to the mall Dad?"

"It sounds like both my girls think that would be a great idea. So sure."

"Okay, I'll call and ask them, thanks dad."

Kourtney was on the phone talking a mile a minute. And I'm thinking how can one little girl make so much noise. Everything can be so exciting to a teenage girl. What will it sound like with three teens in the house, in the car, what was I thinking?

"Dad, Missy can come over, but only if we can come pick her up, please can we go get her? She doesn't live far away."

"Yes Kourtney, we can pick her up in about an hour."

"Thanks dad." Brandon lights up every time she calls him dad, it's a beautiful thing to see. I love that he's such a doting dad.

"Are you ready for a fulltime family and all the activities involved with a teenage girl?"

"Brandon, with you by my side, I can be ready for anything, right? I was a teen age girl once, long ago but I can still remember what it's like to be a teen."

"Okay babe, just checking on my girl."

"I grabbed Brandon's hand tightly and whispered in his ear, "sweetheart, I am not your girl! I am your woman, a big difference and don't forget that."

He grabbed my other hand as I was letting his hand go and pulled me to his ear and whispered, "I never forget you are my woman! I love every womanly part of you. We will have our private time together later. Kourtney will be in her girlfriend world, and we will be non-existent unless she needs money, or the house is on fire."

I laughed out loud, "Does that happen often around your house?"

"What, the house being on fire?"

"No, I mean, is she used to you being in your bedroom with a woman when she has friends over?"

"No sweetie, just with you in our bedroom, only you. I didn't bring women to the house; I had a daughter to protect."

Hum, I don't know if I believe that or not, but since I'm feeling newly engaged and forgiving, I'm just going to let that story slide.

"You want anything while I'm out picking up girls?" I just raised my eyebrow at Brandon, and he laughed. "That didn't sound right, but you know what I meant."

"Yes, I know what you meant. Brandon, don't you think the girls will want junk food to eat while they are here watching movies and talking about boys? Do you have popcorn, sodas and donuts for breakfast? Young girls don't do healthy in the morning they do yummy and comfort food."

"We have eggs and ham so I could fix them a healthy breakfast if they want it in the morning. We will play it by ear. But thanks for the suggestions. I'll have Kourtney pick out some girl food for their movie time together. They may sleep in till lunch time anyway we'll have to wait and see about what time we head to the mall."

"Drive safe and I'll see you all when you get home. Love you."

It didn't seem like they were gone long at all, but it could have been because I was still unpacking clothes and hanging them up in my closet and with one arm in a cast, my shoulder was killing me from just hanging up clothes. I guess the repetitive motion was what was causing pain in my shoulder.

I heard the girls come in the house, all talking at the

same time and laughing, so much noise and giggling. I came out of my room quickly to meet them and for introductions. The girls were sweet, and I was glad to see Kourtney had such great girlfriends. I have a handful of close girlfriends that I trust completely. A good girlfriend is like a sister, a best friend. But there are a lot of girls out there that are insecure, jealous and mean. I will be on the watch for those "friends" for Kourtney.

My Wisconsin teacher friends are like sisters to me too. A good friend is a gift from God and I'm so glad Kourtney has girls that know how to be good friends. Growing up my best friends were always boys. I've always loved and appreciated boys. I guess growing up the only girl in the family, you learn to relate to them. I'm probably weird but that's how it was for me growing up and that's my comfort zone.

Kourtney's friends had chick flicks playing and Brandon was popping their popcorn so they were ready for their girls' night and we were ready to go upstairs for our evening together. We told the girls if they needed anything to holler and we'd be here, but not to leave the house and no boys.

I just laughed and grabbed a couple of Diet Dr. Peppers and went upstairs. I came into the room and Brandon said, "lock the door and I'm saving you a place right here next to me in bed."

He's so cute, I couldn't resist. We were in our bedroom and starting to get frisky on the bed and Brandon caressed my shoulder and I moaned in pain. Brandon backed off immediately.

"What's wrong? Why are you in pain?"

"My shoulders are really sore from lifting my arm repeatedly over and over all day long and hanging up my clothes in our closets. I know that doesn't even make sense, but it really hurts. Would you try to very carefully massage them to see if it will help?"

"Sure babe, so sorry you are in pain. I might have some gel to put on sore muscles if my massage isn't enough. Then we can resume our earlier activities that were starting to take place right here in our bed."

It took the massage and heating gel for sore muscles, and I started feeling much better and even a little naughty for having sex with him when his daughter and her friends were just down stairs. I'm an adult I don't have to be a good girl anymore.

I love my future husband. Not to kiss and tell but he is a giving lover, tender, passionate, strong but gentle too. I'm a very lucky woman. He's such a good kisser, seriously curl your toes and roll your eyes back in your head great kisser! His lips are so full and tender, simply heaven!

After our love making, Brandon asked, "When do you want to tell your family about our engagement and when do you want to get married?"

I told him, "I don't want a big wedding, just a small intimate gathering maybe at our house and then off to a beach somewhere beautiful. This will be my third wedding and I would be fine to skip the whole big wedding thing completely if that's what you want. What do you want Brandon, this is your wedding too? Don't you think our beginning together should be what we both want? Do you want a big wedding?"

"Jenna, I would be fine to go to a justice of the peace or Vegas. I don't really care about the big expensive wedding. What I do know is that I want to see you walk down an aisle, to me, only me, and say "I do" in front of our family and closest friends. That's what I want."

"Okay now that we've decided on a small intimate wedding, what location?"

"It's your turn to go first this time, where do you want to be married?"

"Well, my first wedding was in a church, to Tom. My second wedding was outside at a beautiful park, with Jacob.

How about my third and last wedding jumping out of an airplane? Just kidding, and the look on his face was totally worth that comment. Seriously how would you feel about marrying me on a beautiful beach? I've never had a beach wedding, and I love the ocean. What do you think about that sweetheart?"

"A beach sounds hot, like my soon to be wife. I'll marry you on a beach any day babe!"

"Okay, we have a small wedding on the beach and now where for the honeymoon? We will already be on a beach, but I don't want to honeymoon with my family. I just want you and only you. I don't want to sound selfish, but I will share your love for the rest of my life with your daughter, and I'm fine with that, it's the way it should be. But on my honeymoon, I don't want to share you with anyone. Just you and me. Still love me?"

Brandon was grinning adoringly and said "more than ever lover! What's left to decide?"

We need to determine which beach we will be united on and set the official date for our wedding. Oh and our honeymoon location too.

"Jacob and I went to Bora Bora, and it was off the charts amazing."

"I've never gone there before, but since you've been there recently, maybe we could pick another place."

"Good point, you're right."

"How about Hawaii?"

"I went there with Tom."

"I hope we run out of husbands before we run out of islands."

"Very funny."

Then we came up with the perfect honeymoon destination, Bermuda. Because we were sort of in a love triangle and Bermuda triangle, seemed to be a good fit for us. We just laughed and said that's perfect, Bermuda here we come.

All we need to do is to set the date for our wedding. Brandon didn't want his daughter living with some guy before she gets married, so he wanted us to have a quick wedding. I'm fine with that too.

We love each other and we are together anyway, so I'm fine to marry this summer. I'd be a June bride, now the hard part was going to be telling my family. I hadn't met Brandon's extended family yet, so that should be fun. I figured if I could win over Jacob's family, I could handle Brandon's with no problem. Boy, was I in for a surprise!

The next afternoon, while Miss. Kourtney and her friends Beverly and Missy shopped in every store at the mall, I had my coffee and sat in a comfortable chair at the mall and called my mom and brother. I filled them in on what I'd been up to and my engagement news.

Mom was cautious and told me not to be in such a hurry for love. I told her I wasn't the time keeper in my life. I just had to follow my heart and Brandon was a good man and shockingly enough, he loves me, and I love him. We're getting married in June and honeymooning in Bermuda.

Mom said let her know the date and the colors and she'll start shopping for a dress. I told her we were going to marry on a beach, and everyone was going to wear white and have a dinner at an upscale hotel at their airconditioned banquet room for our family and guests.

Mom said she would be there and loved me and was happy that I was happy and healthy. She asked me if I'd heard from or about Jacob. I told her all that had happened since the divorce, including the goodbye letter. She was glad he was getting help and said she couldn't believe how much Jacob ended up being like Tom.

I told her I didn't want to go down that road. It's a dead end for me. She changed the subject and said that Jeff liked Brandon. And he would be very excited that the two of us were finally together.

After I got off the phone with mom, I threw away my

empty cup and got back in line to order another coffee. I knew I would require more caffeine to navigate this conversation with my brother. I had texted him earlier to ask when a good time was to have a conversation. He texted back the time, so at the prearranged time, I called Jeff

He couldn't believe that I was already with Brandon.

"I like Brandon, but you need to slow down. This is happening way to fast."

"Time won't change my feelings. Mark the second Saturday in June for my wedding. I'm going to be a June bride, on the beach.

"Well at least you won't have to look for a dress. You can pick from the two you already have."

"Ha, very funny Jeff, and no pink for this wedding everyone is wearing white but me. "

"Jenna, I'm your brother and I love you, but you jump from one man to another, non-stop. You are feast or famine. You need a reality check. You need to be happy with yourself first, not look for happiness in every man that asks you to marry him.

You can say no, or later dude. You don't have to marry every man you sleep with it's the twenty-first century. Couples are more progressive."

"Jeffrey Scott, I'll have you know I couldn't sleep with a man I didn't love. I'm not a ho-ho you know. I'm positive that I've slept with fewer men than you have slept with women, if you want to have this conversation. I just must have a large capacity to love." Jeff and I both started cracking up after I said that.

"Seriously, I love Brandon, he's been nothing but wonderful always. He has no mental illness in his family and has been with me through the loss of my baby, a divorce…"

"WAIT Jenna, did you say you were pregnant?"

"Oh yeah that was a nightmare for us to get through, but

Brandon was by my side and was supportive and happy about our future. I'm the one who broke his heart; I'm the one who ran away with Jacob. And Jeff before you say anything about Jacob, honestly, I loved Jacob and part of my heart always will.

But all things considered, Brandon is the man I want to grow old with, he's really the "one" for me, till death parts us, my heart has found its forever home. No more back and forth between two men. He's the one."

"I'm sorry to hear about you losing your baby. You know your doctor brother here wants to know all the details, but the brother part of me will let you leave that part in the past if you are sure you are okay."

"Sweetheart, I am healthy, other than a couple of broken bones from my recent near death car wreck. I am fine physically and emotionally. Are you going to give me away again?"

"If this is for the last time, then I'll give you away. I'll have to tell Brandon about the no return policy on you."

"Yes, you do that."

"Jenna, just so you know couples get counseling if they have marriage problems, divorce isn't always the answer. I love you and want you to be happy, but your choices have been terrible with men. I hated Tom, and Jacob wasn't as bad as Tom, but I didn't want you to marry him either. What I know of Brandon, I like. But I don't know him well enough yet to know any differently. And Jenna, you don't know him well enough to marry him yet either. "

"Alright then, how long should I live with him before you think I should marry him? Six months, one year, two, five years how long should I live in sin with the man I love to be the magic number for you to feel good about me remarrying? Time just measures time. People change and I want to grow and change with Brandon committed to me, and me to him.

I really want you to be supportive of Brandon and me,

but I understand your reluctance with my history, I really do. I would love for you to trust me, but if you don't, you don't. Dad's not here to walk me down the aisle, and if you don't feel comfortable in that role, I will ask someone else. I just love you the most in this world and wanted you to be part of our special day.

I don't want you to feel any pressure. I will love you the same if you do or don't walk me down the aisle. You're my brother. If Brandon can trust me with his love and his daughter's love, then I hope in time you will be able to have enough love to support me and my fiancé."

"Okay, it's just I never know what I'm going to hear when you call. It's always on a scale of emergency status and it's hard for me to keep up with you."

"No, please don't say I'm high maintenance and all drama, I got all those comments from Jacob, and those wounds are still very hurtful and fresh. I don't want to feel like I can't tell you everything because you'll think its drama or intense. I'm sort of crying inside right now that you said that to me. I can't help some of the things that have happened to me. Some of this mess I created myself with bad choices. And I'll own those bad choices.

But that's all in the past. I love you and I'm getting married. I hope you can support us in the future. You will have plenty of time to adjust to me and Brandon when you see us together. I love you bro, but I've got to go, I'm at the mall with Brandon and his daughter. I'm sitting with a coffee and trying not to be emotional.

They are shopping and I see Brandon walking toward me. Let's change the subject. What's going on in your life? Let me guess you work all the time, and the boys are full time into their sports and your beautiful wife is busy making business deals and kicking butts."

"You pretty much covered all the bases and you're right on all accounts."

"Facebook pictures keep me up to date with your

darlings. Well give my love to the family and I hope to see you in June."

"Yes, I'll be there for you. Sorry if I was rough on you, I just love you and I have to run at full speed to keep up with your everchanging life. We are good sis. I'll talk to you later! One more thing, stay out of trouble and try not to break any bones between now and the wedding!"

I laughed, "You do realize I don't actually try to break my bones it just happens. But I will make an extra effort to not be klutzy between now and the wedding," and I hung up the phone.

The girls were still shopping and Brandon walked back to me from the book store where he was looking at photography books. They wouldn't let me take my coffee into the bookstore, but they sell coffee in the bookstore, make any sense to you? So, I sat in the mall's courtyard coffee shop's comfy oversized chair, and Brandon came over to check on how I was doing.

He came walking my way with his handsome sexy smile and I had no choice but to stand up and kiss my man. I forgot we were in public, in our town, I just saw the man I loved and wanted to show him how much he meant to me. He just smiled and asked if he could sit for a minute. I said sure.

We sat down and he wanted to know how our news went over with my family. I told him mom was fine, considers you family already and can't wait to get to know Kourtney when and if she wants another Grandma. Kourtney will be the only granddaughter my mom has, so she is already excited to spend time with her to get to know her.

Jeff on the other hand, is more cautious. He did not like Tom or Jacob, so he's questioning my ability to choose a husband wisely. I told him the heart wants what the heart wants. I think he'll come around, but if he doesn't, I will marry you anyway; I'll just have to find someone else to walk me down the aisle.

I was tearing up, so I had to stop and take another drink of my almost empty cup of coffee. I spoke again in a quieter tone and said that I hate that you will never know my dad. I'm pretty sure Jeff will walk me down the aisle. Jeff is big hearted and a great protective brother.

Brandon took my hand and said, "Jenna, I'm sorry this is hard for you. Babe I will walk down the aisle with you, and we will meet the pastor together, we can just do things different this time. It's our wedding after all; we can do what we want to. Would that make it easier for you?" (Great I'm at a mall surrounded by people and I just want to cry. If I can't even walk down the aisle by myself, on my own two feet, maybe I'm not ready to get married yet. Maybe I should wait a while. But no, I don't want to wait. I'm getting married in June.)

"Thank you for that sweet offer, you are always so thoughtful. But I want to walk down the aisle to you and see the look on your face. I want to look into your eyes and read what your handsome face is saying without words. I hope and pray you will be conveying to me with your eyes and facial expressions that you are glad to be spending forever with me.

That you think I look beautiful and that you want me as your wife forever and always. That's the look I want to see on your face when I'm walking down the aisle, away from all my past mistakes and to you, my future. I love you."

"Wow, I don't even have words to say after that. I love you too." There is no way we are writing our own vows because after what you just said, my words would pale in comparison!" He smiled his handsome grin, squatted down next to me, in my chair in the middle of the mall, and kissed me like he meant it.

When we finished with our coffee, Brandon found a shop he thought I might want to explore. We walked hand and hand into the Bridal shop to look and see if anything jumped out at us. One of the store clerks asked if I had been into her shop before, and I said, "yes about two years ago." I had looked in her store when I was with Jacob, but I didn't buy from this store.

I was impressed that she would remember me, so she helped me look at dresses for a June wedding. I did find a dress that was very pretty lots of pearls and dainty sparkling white beads and it was a light shade of off-white but not an old antique color, just slightly off from bright white. I think that would be perfect for a third marriage.

It was a straight cut dress and down to my knees. It was sleeveless and had intricate beading on the breast section. I wanted to try it on, but not with Brandon here, I wanted to see it on first. It was difficult with my arm cast but not too bad since it didn't have sleeves to mess with and the leg cast wasn't a problem because the dress wasn't to the floor. Brandon said we had plenty of time to go try on dresses, so I went back and tried it on.

It was even prettier on than it was on the hanger. I really wanted Brandon to see it, to get his opinion. I asked the girl to bring him back to the dressing room. I asked Brandon if he wanted to see me in the dress before our wedding, or if he wanted to see it for the first time with me walking down the aisle?

He said now if I wanted him to see it. I let him into the huge, mirrored dressing room. He just stared at me, I had my hair pulled up in a pair of beautiful pearl clips, and my back side was open to my low back in a v-shaped covered with a very fine mesh that looked really romantic.

I looked at Brandon in the mirror and he spoke soft and quiet when he said, "you've never looked more beautiful." I think he had tears in his eyes. He thought we should buy it because it fit like it was made for me, very form fitting, the arms, the breast area, the waist curved in to fit. The length was flattering too, everything was just perfect and different than any dress I'd ever been married in before.

Brandon said, "Sold Sweetheart." He stepped out to buy the dress. I was carefully getting out of the dress. I really liked the dress and couldn't believe that we found the perfect dress so quickly, but when you find the one, you just know it. We walked out of the store with the dress in plastic garment bag and hanger and the girls found us coming out of the store.

Kourtney wanted to see the dress and I told her she'd see it before the wedding. but it was in its storage bag to protect it and I wanted to keep it stain free until the wedding. She said that would be fine. She couldn't wait to see it and what she could see, looked beautiful.

She and her friends wanted to eat in the mall commons area so the bridal shop ladies told us they would hold my dress at the shop until we were ready to leave the mall. We thanked them and told them we'd be back for our dress in an hour or two.

We headed to the food court to grab a bite to eat. The girls wanted us to save a table while they got plates of food and brought them over to Brandon and me. Brandon had a couple of men come up and talk with him and they were laughing and visiting. so I just sat and drank my Diet Dr. Pepper and had a few bites of his food, I wasn't really hungry when the food arrived, it just didn't look good to me.

After lunch was over, Brandon put his arm around me and in his other arm was carrying my dress to the car. I love him. I see the other women look at him when we walk by, and I don't blame them because he is a looker! I love him and he loves me and I'm marrying him. I can't believe I haven't thought of Jacob since my brother mentioned his name. I'm so happy and it's all because of Brandon and our life together.

Brandon told his family that he proposed and that we are getting married in June. His mom and dad who have always been married to each other said they'd be coming to visit next weekend to meet me and spend some time to allow me to get to know them.

I said, "That's fine, I would love to get to know your folks, and to hear stories about you when you were younger. I am looking forward to meeting them too."

Brandon told Kourtney, "Your Grandma and Grandpa are coming to visit next weekend."

"Okay dad, then can I stay at moms' next weekend?"

I just looked at her in shock. I wondered why she wouldn't want to spend time with her grandparents that she never gets to see. Brandon looked at my surprised expression and said, "My mom is more of an acquired taste."

"Good to know. How much does she know about me?"

"Everything, you don't have the market on the truth you know."

"That's fine, I just wondered what I'd be dealing with, that's all."

CHAPTER 18

The In-laws

The week flew by, and I was all unpacked and integrated into Brandon's home and daily life. Friday night was finally here, and we heard his parents knocking on the door. Brandon answered the door and they were hugging one another and genuinely happy to see him. "Kourtney is at her mom's house tonight but will join us for lunch tomorrow." Then there was me and my casts coming down the stairs to greet them.

Brandon's dad gave me a big hug and said, "welcome to the family."

His mom hugged me and said, "Glad to finally meet you after all this time. We've heard so much about you."

"Glad to meet you too. Come on in and we can relax in the den." Brandon carried their luggage into the guest bedroom, and I offered drinks and refreshments. They drank water, healthy like their son, and I had my soda of choice and we sat down to visit. The mom, Brooklyn was full of questions, and not many smiles came my way. I felt like some of her questions were prying, but I didn't want to be rude to her.

After the third question that I felt was out of bounds, Brandon spoke up, "Mom, Jenna's not on trial here, she is my fiancée and I love her. She is perfect for me. Kourtney adores her too."

Brooklyn said, "I'm just worried that being married twice before is a bad example for our Kourtney. "Marriage is hard work, not just something you run away from when things get tough like she's done twice before. We are a family that works at what's important."

She had pushed me to my limit, so I said, "I'm so glad we got to meet, and I've had an exhausting day, so if you don't mind, I'll excuse myself. I'm sure you would love some one-on-one time with your son. I'll see you all in the morning."

Brandon excused himself for a minute and walked me to our room. "I'll be back downstairs in a moment." His dad already had the television remote in hand and was trying to find the news.

His mom was up looking around the house like I might have stolen something. Before I could leave the room Brooklyn, asked "Brandon, do you and Jenna have a picture that I could take to put in our local paper in the engagement section? If you plan on going through with this wedding, I need a picture."

She mentioned that they live in a small town and said it would mean so much to her if I would give her a picture.

I told her, "I know a great photographer and maybe he will take our picture for an engagement photo." Then I winked at Brandon and walked up stairs shaking my head. Brandon ran after me, chasing me up the stairs and smacking my butt cheeks like they were drums. I entered the bedroom in disbelief. "Why in the world did you do that when you know your mom was watching?"

"That's exactly why I did it! I laughed out loud, but you

are just so cute, I couldn't keep my hands off you."

"I'm sorry your mom and I aren't hitting it off like I hoped we would. I wanted her to relax and know that you love her and I'm not trying to take her place in your life. I don't want to be your mom I want to be your lover and friend and soon to be wife. She needs mom time, to tell you what you should do and talk you out of marrying me.

And you should listen to your mom. It's not too late to call the whole thing off if you want that. I love you, but more than my happiness, I want you happy, long term happy. Family is very important to both of us, and I know you won't be truly happy if your family isn't happy about us too."

"Don't even kid around about us not being together. I lost you once and it isn't going to happen to me ever again! I mean it! I love you, and you and Kourtney, we are my family. Babe I know you love me, and I love you too. I'll go down and spend time with my folks. Mom will come around it just takes her time. Remember, she's an acquired taste."

"Thank you, I think I stopped breathing for a minute there, I need to sit down. I want you to have a good relationship with your mom. She loves you, and they say the way a man treats his mom is the way he will treat his wife. So love her, respect her and be kind to her. You don't have to agree with her, but always make her feel welcome in our home. Thank you for standing up for me downstairs when she was crossing the line.

I adore you for that, I counted on you having my back and you didn't let me down, you were there for me. I plan on showing you how much I appreciate your support down there when you come back to bed tonight. Now I'll get in the shower and relax while you are down stairs getting tied into knots. Not fair, but what's family for (I said laughing)?"

Brandon kissed me, and whispered, "enjoy your shower,

I hope I won't be late, but my mom is a talker. I heard what you just said, and I love you more than I could ever imagine. Instead of focusing on how critical my mom was to you, you were thinking about me and my long-term relationship with my mom. That is one of the many reasons why I love you so completely. You are a wonderful woman just by being you, and I don't tell you enough how wonderful you are, I love you sweetheart, I'll see you in a bit."

"Thank you and enjoy your time with your parents. Don't worry about me up here naked and alone, I'll be here when you get ready for bed."

"I'm looking forward to that as always my dear." And with that, Brandon shut the bedroom door and headed downstairs. I just smiled and headed to the bathroom.

My phone buzzed telling me I had a text message. It was a message from Kourtney, she said, "Hey Jenna, just checking to see if you were still breathing after Grandma chews you up and spits you out. She's always like that, so don't take it personally. I'll be there tomorrow and when Grandma sees how happy we are together, she will mellow out. Love you Kourtney"

I had to text her back immediately, "Sweetheart, I love you so much. I miss you and thank you so much for your kind supportive words. I look forward to being with you tomorrow and hope you can enjoy your short visit with your Grandma and Grandpa while they are here. Love you too, Jenna."

Brandon came up several hours later and I was lost in a good book. I had no idea he'd been down there so long. He came in quiet and wasn't very talkative. "Hi babe, you okay?"

"Yes, I'm just really tired. Do you mind if I just take a shower and we visit in the morning?"

"Of course not, that's fine. I'll stop reading when you get in bed." He went to the bathroom brushed his teeth and came to bed. No hugging, kissing, nothing. What did his mom say to him? He came to bed, so I turned off the lights and he pulled me next to him, his arms around my middle and I just scooted against him closed my eyes and went to sleep. No place would I rather be than safe and sound in his arms.

Our alarm hadn't even gone off yet, and his mom was standing next to me in our bedroom. No knock on the door, just walk in like she owned the place. "Brandon my sweet and Jenna dear, so sorry to wake you up, but I don't know how to work your coffee machine and your father wants his coffee. Are you two getting up anytime soon? We can go out for breakfast if you don't want to fix something here, we don't want to be an imposition." I looked at the alarm clock, it said 6:11.

Brandon reassured his mom. "Mom, I'll be down in a minute, and we can have breakfast here." I sat up in bed and when she left the room, Brandon shut our bedroom door behind her and I got up threw on my sweats, pulled my hair back into a ponytail, brushed my teeth then went downstairs to join the family for breakfast.

Brooklyn was quick to say, "dear you can go back to bed if you want, I'm sure you don't usually get up this early since you don't have a job."

I replied, "Oh, do you work outside of the home?"

"No, I'm retired."

"What was your profession?"

"I was a librarian."

"That is so interesting. Who are some of your favorite authors?"

"Oh dear, I don't like to talk shop. Are you going to be joining us for breakfast?"

"I had planned on it, is there a reason why I wouldn't join my fiancé and his parents for breakfast?"

"It's just that you are so thin, I just didn't think that you would be the type to eat three meals a day."

"I eat every day but thanks for the compliment." I changed the subject and the focus off of me and started talking to Brandon's dad, "Are you a coffee drinker? How do you take your it?"

"Black, with one ice cube."

"Coming right up!" I went to the coffee machine and Brandon was fixing egg whites, mushrooms, onions, and tomatoes to make egg omelets. I toasted the bread and set the table. I poured juice and we all sat down together and ate by 6:30 a.m. on a Saturday morning.

"What time will we see Kourtney?"

"She should be here around noon."

Brandon's dad asked, "Are there any good golf courses open today that he could hit a few rounds before Kourtney gets here?"

"Let me make some calls, we may be able to get a tee-time. I'll call right now." I think Brandon had to pay a high price to do this for his dad, but his dad didn't seem to appreciate his effort, just hurry up Brandon we don't want to be late for our tee-time at 8:30. I want to be back before Kourtney to welcome her home." Brandon looked at me like I was an afterthought and I could see his wheels turning. You alone with my mom for the whole morning, it finally registered with him.

"Jenna, mom, why don't you two come with us and watch us play. We'll get a cart and the four of us could play."

Brooklyn said, "Sure, that would be fun. Jenna, do you play?"

"No, I don't, but I'd love to go and watch Brandon play."

I opened the front door to see the temperature and I heard his mom comment, "Is she going to wear that out in public Brandon?"

I turned around and said "No mam; I was just checking the temperature so I would know what I should wear. We can leave the dishes for when we get back. Meet you all back downstairs in 10 minutes and we'll leave in 15 minutes."

Brandon and I rushed up stairs. He jumped into the shower and I threw on a checked pair of shorts that came down to my mid-thighs, and a light pink oxford short sleeved shirt and comfortable tennis shoes and a light pink and green checkered jacket that matched my shorts for the preppy outing we were about to embark on.

"I didn't know you golfed."

"I don't golf very often but have a membership for the rare occasion I need to have a membership for family or friends. Dad enjoys it, so I do it to spend time with him."

"I see."

"What do you see?"

"I see you love your dad and pulled strings to get him a Saturday tee-time at the last minute and he didn't even thank you. I see that you are a good and loyal son and I'm proud of you."

"Thanks, you ready to go?" I threw on my make-up, and some perfume, brushed my teeth again and we headed down the stairs. His dad looked excited, and his mom just looked bored.

Brooklyn and I sat in the back and the men sat up front as we drove to the nicest course in town. We got to Thousand Oaks Golf Resort, and there were lots of people, mostly men, out already swinging at golf balls. It was fun to see Brandon and his dad play.

Brandon let me swing a couple of his shots and I didn't do terrible. I did take lessons once from a semi-pro golfer but didn't really get the fun part of golfing. I stopped going. Besides that, it was expensive.

We spent the morning together and he and his dad joked around, his dad was laughing and having a great time. Brooklyn seemed to be warming up to me. Then when it was just her and I alone on the golf cart and the boys were on the green almost within ear shot she said, "Jenna can I speak frankly with you?"

"I didn't know you knew another way."

She retorted "You are not good enough for my son. I love Brandon, and you broke his heart when you said you'd marry him then left him and married another man. What kind of woman does that to someone she says she loves? I don't think you are all that pretty, so you must be really experienced in the bedroom."

I couldn't even speak. Brandon saw my distressed face and walked over to us quickly. He asked, "What's going on here ladies?"

I told him "Well your mom just gave me a compliment. She thinks I must be really good in bed because I'm not that pretty."

Brandon just looked at his mom. "Mom why did you say that?"

"I didn't say those exact words."

"Mom?"

"Well, I sort of said that, but I didn't know she was going to be a tattletail too."

"Grow up! I love her and I'm marrying her. If you want to be part of our life, be nice, if you don't want to be part of our life, keep up this behavior. You understand this is a done deal?"

"Yes, I understand, you are taking this sluts side over your own mother. I can't believe you would treat me this way. Picking her over family!"

"I can't believe you are being so rude calling her names being so unkind. Respect is earned mother, and you need to step up your game in that area. Dad's calling and it's my turn, so be nice and let's have a pleasant day, shall we?"

I just smiled and walked over with him to the green. I didn't want to be anywhere near his mom, and he just stood up to his mother for me and called her on what was inappropriate yet left the door open for her to turn things around to have a good day.

He's such a good man, just another confirmation that he is the one. I am going to marry this man and make him proud of me and make his mom regret the doubting and unkind words she had at the beginning of our life together. I walked to the golf cart with the men and Brandon's mom said, "Jenna, I'm sorry, I was out of line, please forgive me."

"Thank you for your apology. We all want the same thing, for Brandon and Kourtney to be happy and healthy. I want to make him happy that's what makes me happy. I love your son."

Brandon reached over grabbed me and kissed me like he usually does when no one is looking. So it felt good to love the man who gives me purpose and strength. Then Brandon said, "Oh and mom, just for the record, she is good in bed." I hit Brandon in the arm and his dad started cracking up. His mom immediately turned red and looked away.

Before we got to the next green, we were all laughing out loud. Brandon knows his family and knows how to communicate effectively. I just stayed close to my man and let him pave the way for me and our future with his family. We made it home in time to see Kourtney's mom drop her off at the driveway. Brooklyn went out to talk to the ex-wife and they talked at the end of the driveway for quite a while.

Kourtney said, "Thanks for the text." Brandon just looked at me. I told him his beautiful daughter sent me a text last night and it was so meaningful to me I had to text her back. I gave her a big hug and kiss. "Love you Miss. Kourtney."

"Love you to Ms. Jenna. What's for lunch I'm starving. Mom said I slept too late that I'd have to wait and have an early lunch with Grandma and Grandpa. Are you guys hungry? You are going with us, right?"

"We had breakfast at 6:30 so it's almost 12:00, I could

eat again. What do you want for lunch?"

"Grandma likes that place that is a cafeteria that you go through with a tray and pick each individual item."

"That's so sweet of you Kourtney, to think of what your grandparents would like to eat, instead of what you want. You are such a mature young lady."

"Do you like that place Jenna?"

"I've never been, but if your grandparents like it, I'm good to go."

"Just to let you know," Kourtney whispered in my ear, "It's kind of an old peoples place to eat." Grandpa Jon came over and was the doting affectionate Grandpa on his Granddaughter. They sat on the couch and were talking like a couple of school girls. It was so cute to sit back and watch.

I watched Brandon, and he's so proud of his beautiful daughter. I just stood next to Brandon and took his hand. He took his thumb and gently rubbed the top part of my hand. I can't wait to marry him.

We got into the car and headed to Tater Tot's Cafeteria for lunch. Kourtney was correct the place was full of older people, but there were some younger families too. They had a big variety of food choices. They all looked good and from what I ate, it was delicious. Now I'm a little sad that it's an old person's place to eat, because I want to come back, yum, yum.

I made sure to eat lots of food so his mom could see I eat three good meals a day. I figured I ate healthy for breakfast, so lunch could be food I like, comfort food. Kourtney was sitting between her grandparents and talking non-stop as her usual self. I just ate and appreciated her taking the heat off me for a few moments.

Then I heard Brooklyn ask Kourtney, "So dear, what do you think of your dad's fiancé'?"

I smiled at Kourtney and Kourtney looked back at me. Then she said, "Grandma, I hate her, she's spends all dads' money, and she has men at the house when dad's gone all the time."

I couldn't believe she was saying this. I looked at Brandon in shock and she and he just burst out laughing. Brooklyn and I both didn't think that it was funny. But I'm sure the shocked looks on our faces was comical.

When Kourtney finally stopped laughing, she said, "Honestly, I love Jenna, she is great. She's kind and a good listener, but the best part of Jenna is that she loves my dad and he loves her. What do you think Grandma?"

Brandon and I just looked at her and she said, "I think you are right Kourtney." Brandon patted my leg under the table and I started breathing again. I think I'd been holding my breath because it took me several breaths to get my heart rate back to a calm pace. Lunch was over and we still had the day to deal with Brooklyn.

Kourtney wanted her Grandma to help her pick out fabric to make a quilt for a school project. Jon and I stayed home while Brandon took his mom and Kourtney fabric shopping.

Jon told me privately, "Sorry that my wife was so protective of Brandon, but you held your own with her. You fit in with the family just fine. You are very pretty, and Brandon is a lucky man."

"Thank you for your kind and meaningful words."

"I'll have to deny everything I just said if you ever mention this conversation to my wife." I just laughed at him. "Do you mind if I watch the golf channel?"

"Not at all." I poured him a cup of coffee with one ice cube. He smiled knowing I remembered how he liked it. I told him, "I have a headache, so I am going to take a nap until the others get home. If you need anything be sure and make yourself at home and holler if you need something. I'd be glad to assist."

I went upstairs to my bedroom locked the door and went to sleep. I woke up to a knocking on my bedroom door.

"Jenna?"

"Yes honey, just a minute." With two casts it took me a minute to get out of bed. It was Brandon and he looked puzzled.

"Why did you lock the bedroom door?"

"I was home alone with a man in the house and I was going to sleep, I don't mean anything against your dad, I just did it without thinking."

Brandon smiled, "Good practice to get into, the only man in our bedroom is me."

"That's what I'm talking about. How was your shopping?"

"Mom wants a nap and to be honest so do I. Kourtney is down stairs playing checkers with dad. Set the alarm and I'll join you."

"I don't know why I'm so tired, but I could sleep for another hour if you are next to me." He set the alarm and we slept.

We got up and I felt much better. We went downstairs to clean up breakfast dishes and to start on dinner plans. We grilled chicken, put rice and vegetables in the steamer I fixed lemon bars for desert. Dinner was a big success then I taught them a card game called tic, and we laughed and enjoyed our evening together.

His mom wanted us to all go to church together the next day. I thought that was a good idea. We hadn't gone to church together as a family yet and I would love to sit in church with my new family. So after a late night of cards and laughter we went to bed.

Sunday morning Brandon's mom said she didn't feel well and wanted to go home early if that was okay with us. We asked her if she wanted Tylenol or aspirin, but she didn't want to take anything. We helped them pack, gave hugs and told dad to drive safely. They left for home and we went back to bed. We will have to do church as a family soon, because I do want that for Brandon, Kourtney and me.

Brandon and I talked about going to church and he said he'd go with me if it was important to me. I told him I'd really like for us to find a place we both felt at home to meet the pastor and have him marry us. Brandon was supportive and said whatever I wanted he wanted that for me too.

We visited several churches before we found a church that we both liked the music and the pastor, and the people were nice too. You wouldn't think that finding a fit in a church would be difficult, but it was time consuming project for us. We met with the pastor and started pre-marital counseling. I felt comfortable doing this and Brandon was at ease too. We were both honest and it was pretty much a formality so we could get married by Reverend Daryl Gattea.

Kourtney helped me pick out flowers and bridesmaid dress colors. We decided the flowers should be deep corals and bright yellows. I started with the tanning booth and my dress still fit. June was soon approaching and this wedding was really going to happen. I was excited to make this official and have the wedding behind me. I was looking forward to marring Brandon, but I didn't want a big wedding.

Kourtney was my maid of honor and Jeff was walking me down the aisle. Brandon's best friend from childhood was coming to be his best man. I was getting my casts taken off both my arm and my leg in three days. I wanted to surprise Brandon with my casts off. Thank goodness I heal quickly.

I had three weeks to try to get my pale cast side tanned to an even color of the other side of my body. It was a challenge, but I was up for it. I needed to look balanced for my wedding day pictures and honeymoon. I could always do a fake spray tan to even things out if it didn't work.

Chapter 19

Forever

Our rehearsal day was finally here. We decided to have our wedding at the beach in Pensacola, Florida where the sand is white, and the water was crystal clear, and the water is shallow for about a quarter of a mile off the coastline. We had white wooden chairs set out on the beach and underneath an arch of live greenery is where we took our vows.

We had the ultimate backdrop with the setting sun against the crystal blue ocean behind us. Then to add to the senses of vision was the sound of the water's tide flowing in and out, it was a perfect background for us to be in the foreground starting our lives together. It was a small intimate wedding and everyone wore white. Jeff wore white jeans and a deep coral shirt like Brandon's, he looked sharp, as always.

The weather was perfect for our special day. Hot but it was overcast so it wasn't so humid for a June evening in Florida. I felt loved and I was so glad we were starting our lives together in the sight of God, family and friends. Brandon had white tux pants and a blood orange coral long sleeved shirt, it was too hot on the beach for the jacket, and I loved him in the color anyway. It may not sound attractive, but he looked so handsome I couldn't wait to say, "I Do".

It was a beautiful wedding. Walking down the aisle and looking at Brandon's face made all my hopes and dreams come true, without a single word being spoken. I could see it, he wanted me, he loved me, better and worse it was all in his eyes. Maybe because I'd done the wedding thing twice before, but I was relaxed and could really enjoy every part of the service.

Brandon looked so striking, he's so good to me I am a truly blessed woman! I know he couldn't afford the wedding ring as nice as Jacob had bought for me, so we used Jacob's ring as a trade in and I ended up with an over-the-top amazing lifelong beautiful wedding ring.

We went to the hotel for our wedding dinner celebration that had an entire wall overlooking the ocean and there was a live band playing in the bar across the hall from our rented conference room. It was great fun and better yet, we didn't have to pay for the band. We danced and talked and laughed with family and friends until late.

Kourtney looked beautiful in her white dress with coral flowers in her hair. She was so sweet and I'm so glad she enjoyed our wedding too. She was going to spend a couple of days on vacation in Florida with her grandma and grandpa. Then go back with them to spend a week at their house for summer break while we were away on our week-long honeymoon.

We spent our wedding night in the honeymoon suite at the hotel with an unforgettable view of the ocean. We had a passionate first night as Mr. and Mrs. Brandon Johnson. Our flight left the next day at 10:45 a.m. for our week in Bermuda. We were so busy with everything leading up to our wedding, with arrangements with family and verifying that everything was done on the "To do" lists, that when we finally got on the flight to our honeymoon destination, we both slept most of the way there.

Bermuda was as beautiful as all the brochures advertised, the beaches and the sand. But the best part was my beautiful husband. We had an intimate time and it was just a perfect time for us to walk and talk and be together. We didn't fill our time doing excursions all over the island, we decided each day what we were going to do and when we were going to do it. We were on island time, and they are more relaxed, and it was wonderful to absorb some of this culture.

We did a lot of walking and exploring. We walked around touristy places and got stuff to bring home, but mostly just sun, beach, sand, water and lots of fresh fish and fresh fruit. I love eating and living island life. Brandon didn't have any distractions with work, or his daughter, just me, and honestly I loved being the only priority in his thoughts, even if it was only for a week. I wanted to enjoy every moment we had alone together.

I love his daughter, but I'll always wish I hadn't lost our baby. I just pretend Kourtney is mine too. So far, it's working for me; she's Brandon's, so I love her no matter what. I share that part of his love for her and I'm okay with that forever. She is a great kid and I'm proud to be part of her life too.

This honeymoon, I didn't break any bones and we made the most out of every minute of our time together in this beautiful place of the world. We loved the resort, ocean views and explored the island's jungle and waterfalls. We brought our cameras to capture the beauty of this place. We took tons of pictures and enjoyed the ocean swimming and snorkeling.

When we were in the jungle, we paid to climb extremely high towers and then fasten ourselves into harnesses. We glided down a thick cable wire to another tall tower across miles of jungle. It was scary being that high at first, but once I pulled up the courage to jump off the platform, it was a total adrenaline rush. We loved it, and if it wasn't so expensive, we'd have done it over and over. We walked in the jungle on a hiking tour and saw monkeys and all sorts of colorful birds and huge insects.

Brandon is a licensed scuba diver so he did some scuba diving and I did snooba diving since I didn't have my license to scuba dive and didn't want to waste honeymoon time taking classes. I enjoyed my honeymoon time with no regrets.

We took many, stunning pictures of flowers, plants, ocean, and animals. We had a few of us in our pictures too, but it was great to enjoy taking pictures again. It was exciting to go home with not just our private honeymoon memories but pictures of this beautiful area to share with Kourtney and our family and friends too.

It was a gorgeous place, and the people were so friendly I could have stayed two weeks or more, but we had Kourtney coming home so we were anxious to get home to be with our girl. I know she's not my daughter by blood, but I do love her and I'm so glad we have her in our lives.

The week flew by. It felt so good to be away from everything and seeing the beautiful country with my wonderful husband. He tans quickly and my attempts to tan before the wedding helped, but Brandon was as tan as me or maybe even tanner and he didn't fake bake before the wedding, totally not fair, appreciated, but not fair.

We went for a naked swim in the ocean one night in the moon light and it was the sexiest thing I'd ever done. I loved being free, totally free with my husband. During the day you have to be careful because you are so close to the sun here you tan really quickly and he looked hotter than hot with a tan. I couldn't say no to anything he asked or wanted, he was the man I loved and trusted with my life.

My Brandon, my husband, my lover and friend.

Our last day on the island, it was a game changer for us. I think we over did it in the sun the day before and Brandon had a headache, so he was laying down in our bungalow for an early night's rest before our flight back home the next day.

We were packed to leave for the next day and I didn't want to disturb Brandon in our room, but I couldn't sleep, so I walked out of our sliding glass door to the beach and sat in the sand and water and watched the moon rising in the sky and the reflection on the water.

It was a full moon, and it was beautiful. I wanted to remember every sight and sound of this place. It was quiet with the ocean's tide. The beach was empty, and I was just thanking God for not only all my many personal blessings, but the beauty He created around us.

I don't know exactly how long I'd been outside, but the moon was almost centered in the horizon over the ocean, and I'd decided I was ready to go to bed. I started to get up when I saw something move out of the corner of my eye, it was three men, and they were running toward me.

They were between me and my hotel room. I looked behind me and there was no one outside with me only me and three men. I used my outside recess voice and screamed, "Help me Brandon, Help me!"

The men stopped for a moment, and I saw Brandon run out of our room yelling, "Jenna, where are you?" When I saw Brandon, he was behind the men running toward me, so I was in front of the men. I just started running toward Brandon.

The men looked shocked that I had so much volume for such a small figure, but I was scared, and they were still headed toward me. I saw hotel employees running to the beach and lights coming on all over the resort.

The men immediately turned around, ran past Brandon and away from me. Brandon pushed past the men and kept running to me. I collapsed in his arms and just tried to catch my breath and breathe. Brandon was outside in his boxer shorts, and he could have cared less.

"Jenna, what the hell just happened?"

"I couldn't sleep so I wanted to set outside and take in the fresh air and the ocean one more time before we left. I knew you had a headache, I thought I'd be fine to just sit out here for a little while. Then I noticed these men coming toward me, so I started going away from them, but that meant I was going away from you, so all I knew to do was yell and run for you."

"Jenna, thank God you have good pipes! Honey are you okay, you are shaking like a leaf?"

"I'm okay, just don't let go of me Brandon, take me to our room." The hotel workers were to us by this time and Brandon told them that three men tried to attack his wife. They went to report it to their bosses and apologized for the incident. We have a private beach area, but sometimes the locals get in and they said they were so sorry that this had never happened before, and they would notify the authorities right away."

"Boys, we're going back to our room. We will be leaving in the morning."

I was freezing, I think I might have been a little in shock. When we got back to our room, I barely had strength to walk. Brandon turned on the warm water in the tub and I just took off my clothes and sat in the water, which I turned warmer to make it hot.

Brandon was going to join me, but the water was too hot for him, so he was waiting until it cooled some. I just sat there with no words. That could have been such a bad ending to our paradise. But Brandon saved me. The water cooled a bit and Brandon was in the water by my side, holding me, caressing me.

"I was asleep and heard your cry for help. I couldn't get to you fast enough. I could see the men coming toward you, but why did you run toward them?"

"I wasn't running toward them I was running toward you."

"Oh Jenna. Babe you don't understand how beautiful you are. Men are sexual beings; you have to be more careful with midnight strolls without me by your side, okay?"

"I can assure you I won't be going out by myself at night for a long time after this, it really scared me. For a moment there I thought I might not ever see you again, and all I could do was cry out for you." Then the tears finally started falling down my face.

Brandon just held me and told me "It's okay, I'm here and you are okay now." We got out of the hot tub and dried off and went back to bed. Brandon took a couple Tylenol, and then joined me in our bed.

Poor guy he goes to bed with a headache and then is awakened by his screaming wife yelling for him to save her life. Great way to end the honeymoon! We were in bed, I leaned in and whispered his name before he was asleep, "Brandon?"

"Yes babe,"

"Thank you for taking care of me."

He leaned over and whispered back in my ear, "Always!"

I kissed him and we were sharing relief that we still had each other and just the pleasure of being married to a wonderful person. We still have forever together.

We quickly called the front desk to change our wake-up call time to a little later and arranged to take a taxi to the airport to fly home. Then we went off to sleep. The next morning, we jumped in the showers grabbed breakfast and went to check out of the hotel.

I knew that with our location and beautiful honeymoon suite, our bill was going to set us back a few, but when we checked out the manager personally came over to us and said our bill was paid in full and apologized for the incident on the beach last night.

We apprehended the men, and they are not allowed on our beach area again. So sorry for the stress this caused you and your wife. I just looked at Brandon. Who deletes thousands of dollars for a hotel bill like that? Brandon asked if he could have a copy of our room bill saying that the bill was paid in full for our records, and the man just smiled and said of course Mr. Johnson.

Then our taxi arrived, and we were off to our flight home. Brandon called our credit card company to see if this elimination of our hotel bill was legitimate and no false charges made. But they reported our last purchases and it was real. We just had a free honeymoon. We just stared at each other in shock that we didn't have to pay for a week at a four-star rated hotel.

By the time it sank in, we were almost giddy at the airport. What a savings that was for us. I hate that I was scared to death the night before, but I was really glad they deleted our bill, that was so generous of them. The manager hoped we would recommend the place to our friends in the future. We thanked him. Now we are boarding the plane headed home and once again, I'm hungry.

Our flight took off and I had a cup of coffee that was even too strong for me to drink and that is saying something, so then I needed a Diet Dr. Pepper to wash down the thick mud they poured and called coffee. Then the movie started on the flight and Brandon was on his phone checking his mail, calls, etc. Not too long after all the drinks, I needed to use the restroom.

I wasn't thinking and instead of going to the first-class bathroom by our chairs in front of us, I just walked straight back to the back of the plane, a habit, I guess. When I walked back I noticed a man duck his head when I walked past him. I used the restroom and as I was washing my hands, it hit me. I immediately got a sick feeling in the pit of my stomach. The man that ducked down when I walked by, he looked a lot like Jacob. It couldn't be Jacob. He'd be first class or no way. Why would he be on my honeymoon flight home? Was that Jacob?

Oh my gosh, Brandon will get into a fight with him and we'll be kicked off the plane. No way to get home. I have to be smart about my next actions. I have to sit back down in that tiny bathroom and think. I decided I couldn't hide in the bathroom because Brandon would come looking for me and see Jacob, so that plan was a no go.

I came out of the bathroom and walked up to the man I thought was Jacob. I said very quietly, "Jacob, what are you doing here?"

He looked up at me and it was Jacob.

"Jenna, it's not what you think. Andrew told me you were going out of the country and the last time you left the country you were almost eaten by a shark and attacked by a lizard and broke your foot. So, I just wanted to make sure you were okay."

I just shook my head and headed up to the front of the plane to Brandon. Then before I got to my chair, Brandon saw me and I held up one finger to show he'd have to wait a minute, then I went back to Jacob.

"Did you have anything to do with the men on the beach and the paid hotel bill?"

Jacob just looked at the ground and said, "Jenna, they would have never touched you. They had orders from me, and they were not going to lay a hand on you."

"Jacob that is not okay, you have to let me go and you need to talk to your doctor about changing your medications. You can't hire people to scare someone, that's not okay ever Jacob. Just let me go, move on. Please Jacob, please!"

I didn't even let him speak a word, I just turned around and walked up to first class to sit next to Brandon and figure out how I was going to tell him what just happened. I didn't know what Jacob would do, so I had to let Brandon know what I just found out.

I crawled into his lap facing him. My feet were under his legs on the edge of his chair and I was in his face.

"Jenna, what are you doing?"

"I just found out something alarming I have to tell you, and I need you to promise me since we are on a plane over international waters that you will stay calm and think before you react. You promise me, or I can't be honest with you right now."

"I don't know what it is you think you have to tell me, but I've never been out of control or violent so why do you think I would start to act that way now? Just tell me."

The flight attendant walked by and asked me to sit in my seat, and I told her I would in five minutes. So she rolled her eyes at me, and I leaned against Brandon, my breasts against his chest, my head nestled against his neck, and I whispered what I'd figured out and that Jacob had confirmed. Brandon's breathing became rapid and he physically lifted me off his lap and sat me in my chair next to him then he asked in a loud voice,

"Where is he?"

"Brandon please, please, please sit down, don't do this here, you promised me. Wait to confront him until we are on U.S. soil please don't do anything foolish over international waters. He needs medication, he's sick, you aren't, please Brandon." I was grabbing his arms in desperation and tears began to flow. I could see by the look in his eyes, he was going back to confront Jacob.

I just sat back in my chair and let him go. I started praying that God would be with Brandon and Jacob, and that this would end peacefully. He was gone for about five minutes, but I didn't hear any screaming or yelling or announcements for an air marshal, so I was greatly relieved when Brandon was back at my chair motioning for me to move next to the window. He was closer to the aisle, and closer to Jacob if he tried to come up to where we were.

"What happened?"

"I just stood in the doorway where it separates first class from the rest, and I stared at him. I wanted to say so many things, but I knew where it would lead. He's a desperate man to follow his ex-wife on her honeymoon. Jenna, how did he know where we were going? Have you been talking to Jacob?"

That hurt me that he would ask that, "Of course not! I guess he talked to Andrew. I have talked to him, he calls every once in a while to check on me. But I have not talked to Jacob since my hospital room until just now. Do you think I'm playing games with you and Jacob? Is that what you are thinking, oh my God?" I felt sick, not again, a man who doesn't trust me. I couldn't look at him I just sat shaking my head NO.

"No Jenna, look at me, NO! That's not what I think at all, I just couldn't figure out how he knew where we were, that's all. Now I know." I just looked out the window and tried to get myself together. I love Brandon, and my crazy ex-husband went with us on our honeymoon. He is sicker than I thought.

I immediately texted Andrew and told him what happened with Jacob. He followed me on my honeymoon. Then I told him I wouldn't be in touch with him anymore because it's not healthy for me to do that, and I didn't want to put him in a bad situation with his brother.

"Andrew, I love you, but I can't correspond with you anymore. I hope you understood why."

Andrew texted me back, "I'm so sorry, had no idea Jacob would do this. I'm calling Jacob's doctor and texting Jacob to see if he can reason with him."

"Thanks Andrew and good-bye."

What was a relaxing happy honeymoon just 24 hours ago, is now ending in a stressful anxious arrival back home? What is going to happen when we land and Brandon and Jacob are both on U.S. soil, God help us.

"Brandon who are you calling?

"I'm texting my dad to tell him to make sure Kourtney and mom are not at the airport when we land. We will meet them at home. I told dad not to tell anyone, but Jacob was on our flight and landing was going to be rocky."

Dad replied, "Make smart moves son and know your mom and daughter will be at your home when you get here." I don't blame Brandon for wanting to keep Kourtney away from Jacob, but it just makes me anxious wondering what's going to happen when we land.

"Brandon, what you are thinking."

"I need to stay calm, so talking about Jacob and my feelings right now is not a good choice."

"Okay Brandon, I trust you. I know you will make wise decisions for both of us now and when we land. I love you Brandon." I just took his hand in mine. Then I heard the voice over the intercom announcing that we need seat belts on and chairs in the upright positions. We will be landing in the next thirty minutes.

I just looked at Brandon and smiled. He looked at me, no smile, just a hand squeeze then looked out the window. What is going to happen when we land? Jacob was out of line, but he's mentally ill. I was praying silently in my seat that's all I could do. I needed a higher power to make this all better right now.

Time seemed to stand still, ironic since we were still in the air flying. I needed to think about something positive, I don't want to be a basket case by the time I walk off the plane. Brandon, my husband, Brandon think about him. Brandon's hair was bleached out blonder than normal from all the sun and salt I guess, so good looking with his big brown eyes so glad he's mine.

He is such a good photographer, and he was great to help me with my pictures by asking me good questions so I would get the best results with the equator sun glare off white sand and water. He was amazing in all areas of his life, how is that possible? Good professor, great dad and husband. I was so lucky I called him that day for camera advice so I could take his class. Has thirty minutes passed already? Here we go, we're descending, then landing.

My heart was racing, and my palms were sweating. I looked at Brandon and you would never know there was a thing wrong by looking at him. We were in first class so we got to exit the plane first. He stepped back so I could get out into the exit aisle in front of him and he was right behind me. I tried to get Brandon down to the luggage return as soon as possible hoping that our luggage would get out quickly and we wouldn't even have to see Jacob.

But I knew Jacob would be coming to the same location in just moments. I never thought I'd get over my past, and be able to move beyond it, beyond all that pain, all those years are like a distant vapor, just gone. They don't hold any power over me anymore.

Jenna Jamison died in a hospital room she literally no longer exists. I'm just thankful that I somehow found the courage and strength to take the chance to love again and trusted the right man this time because Brandon is worth it all and then some. I have never been happier. My life is complete, and I am so happy to be Mrs. Jenna Johnson.

I know the last name is pretty generic, but I took the name with pride, I feel honored to carry his name, my name, our name. I wonder what adventures Brandon, Kourtney and I will have for our future? I am ready, for anything with my husband by my side. I believe in happily ever after, I'm a hopeful romantic and I'm going to enjoy my husband and our married life forever, or as long as we have together.

I see Jacob coming to where the luggage return is and all I can say is "Please Brandon, please..." Brandon let go of my hand and gently pushed my body behind him.

Jacob walked right up to Brandon and said

"Congratulations Brandon, the best man won. I was out of line this week, and I'm sorry you found out that I was ever there. I just wanted Jenna safe. You won't have to worry about me stocking Jenna anymore. I'll leave you both alone.

I talked to my brother on the phone the last thirty minutes and Andrew helped me see things from a different perspective than I ever thought about, and I'm sorry. You have to take good care of Jenna. I still love her and if she ever calls me, I'll be there so take good care of her!"

"Jacob thanks for your apology, but she is married to me now. She is my wife! And if you ever try to have her kidnapped or fake any kind of pain or injury involving her, I will make sure you never do it again. I don't care how much money you have, that's a promise."

"Is that a threat Brandon?"

"It's the truth Jacob, deal with it. Stay away from Jenna, stay away from me. Get your meds regulated and take your pills every day. We have our luggage. Stay away, go back to Kentucky, you are not welcome in Missouri Jacob. Move on and get your own life."

Brandon took me in one arm and our luggage in the other and we turned our backs to Jacob and walked out of the airport. Jacob behind us and we were moving on. I didn't get a chance to say a word, but Brandon was my defender, and he was the one who laid down the law.

I was very proud of the way he dealt with Jacob. Firm but not overly rude or unkind considering what we'd been through, there isn't anything I would have or could have said that would have been any better than how he dealt with the situation. He's my man, and I love him!

We got back to our car to head for home. I was the first

one to break the silence. "Brandon what are you thinking right now?"

He just looked into my eyes and said, "I'm just wondering if you are worth all this trouble?"

I couldn't believe he said that. "You mean drama don't you Brandon? And what did you decide on your deep thoughts?"

"I think I'll keep you." Then he winked at me to let me know he was teasing me and leaned over and kissed me like a man who was in love. I felt relief that he still wanted me and then enjoyed the taste of his passion and commitment to our marriage.

"I love you too Brandon, only you. Thank you for dealing with my past. Let's go forward to our future." He kissed me one more time then he started my car and we headed for home. Home sweet home! Then our adventures really began.

About the Author

Sonny D. Stone was born and raised in the Midwest. She's lived in rural settings in Kansas and Missouri as well as large cities in Louisiana and Minnesota. She enjoys writing, photography, travel, family, friends and pets. She has a great sense of humor and enjoys many styles of music, and a variety of card games, board and video games and sports. Sonny wanted to share a story of romance and mystery. She had a blast writing this trilogy taking readers on travels with twists and unexpected turns.